BLOTTO, TWINKS AND THE STARS OF THE SILVER SCREEN

The Dowager Duchess of Tawcester knows America is full of wealthy young men, all of whom will fall in love with her daughter, the supremely gifted Twinks — and marriage to a Texan millionaire would solve the Tawcester financial problems once and for all. So, along with trusty chauffeur Corky Froggett, the intrepid Twinks accompanies her brother Blotto on his Californian cricket tour. On arrival in Hollywood, they are invited to a glitzy party where they are introduced to a firmament of Hollywood stars, directors and gossip columnists; but the mood of the party suddenly curdles with the breaking news that beautiful starlet Mimsy La Pim — the (former) love of Blotto's life — has been kidnapped. And Blotto is determined to make it his personal mission to rescue her . . .

Blotto, Twinks

and the

Stars of the
Silver Screen

Simon Brett

ISIS

LARGE
PRINT

First published in Great Britain 2017
by
Constable
an imprint of Little, Brown Book Group

First Isis Edition
published 2018
by arrangement with
Little, Brown Book Group

A catalogue record for this book is available
from the British Library.

ISBN 978–1–78541–498–5 (hb)
ISBN 978–1–78541–504–3 (pb)

Published by
F. A. Thorpe (Publishing)
Anstey, Leicestershire

Set by Words & Graphics Ltd.
Anstey, Leicestershire
Printed and bound in Great Britain by
T. J. International Ltd., Padstow, Cornwall

This book is printed on acid-free paper

To Daisy

who hasn't had a book dedicated to her yet

CHAPTER
ONE

The End of the Season

It was approaching the conclusion of an idyllic September day at the Tawcester Towers cricket pitch. Swallows soared and swooped in the pure blue sky, feeling vaguely that they ought to be migrating southwards soon, but in no hurry to do anything about it. It was one of those perfect English days when nobody feels any great urgency to do anything.

Devereux Lyminster, younger brother of the Duke of Tawcester and known universally as Blotto, sat on the pavilion's veranda sipping iced barley water with one of his old muffin-toasters from Eton, Ponky (whose surname was spelt "L-a-r-r-e-i-g-h-f-f-r-i-e-b-o-l-l-a-u-x" but was pronounced, as everyone who mattered knew, "Larue"). Both of them glowed with the aura of a day well spent.

They had met as boys at prep school, the stage of their education before Eton. Their love of cricket had brought them together. They could still spend whole days, just the two of them, messing around with bat and ball — not practising, of course, British sportsmen thought it rather bad form to practise — but simply having fun throughout the livelong day.

Ponky ran an occasional cricket team, made up mostly of other Old Etonians, and called the Peripherals. Every autumn their final fixture of the season was a match against Blotto's Tawcester Towers XI. And every year the home team won. Though their numbers were made up from supernumerary footmen, estate gamekeepers and under-gardeners, the extraordinary skills of their captain always ensured victory.

Blotto was one of those young men to whom any kind of sporting activity came naturally. Far too much of a gentleman ever to indulge in such below-the-belt activities as training, he just always excelled. So long as there was a ball or a horse involved, he was unbeatable. (When there was anything else involved — like, say, something requiring intellectual effort — Blotto was at the opposite end of the spectrum. Indeed, the more churlish of his acquaintances had been heard to express the view that beneath his golden thatch of hair, behind his honest blue eyes, between his fine patrician ears, there existed a total vacuum. Had Blotto ever heard these unworthy slights, they would have worried him not a jot. Brains, he knew, only complicated things. For the second son of an English Duke in the 1920s, they were completely surplus to requirements.)

Ponky Larreighffriebollaux's congratulations over barley water on Blotto's feats in the field that day — carrying his bat to score two hundred and seventeen out of his team's total of two hundred and eighteen, and taking eight wickets for fourteen runs — were met with characteristic self-deprecation. "Oh, don't talk

2

such meringue, Ponky. Just a few lucky bounces, that's all."

"Well, you say that, but —"

Blotto looked as embarrassed as any Englishman does when confronted by a compliment, and hastily moved the conversation on. "You know, Ponky, this is the time of the year when I always get a strange feeling."

"Oh," said his friend with some surprise. Boddoes who'd been through the same public school rarely spoke about feelings, least of all strange ones. Ponky Larreighffriebollaux wondered whether he was about to be embarrassed.

But the danger passed, as Blotto went on, "I mean, you know, today we've just played a spoffing good game of cricket, Tawcester Towers is looking like one of those landscapes by Sargent . . . or was it Constable . . .? I don't know, one of those natty brush-wielders who's named after a police-wallah . . . and God's in his heaven and all's tickey-tockey with the world."

Ponky could not argue with these sentiments.

"And yet," Blotto continued in an uncharacteristically thoughtful tone of voice, "I can't help feeling there's a bit of a cloud over the sun."

Ponky looked upwards. "No, there isn't," he said. "Blue from horizon to horizon."

"I didn't mean the real sun. Or a real cloud, come to that."

"Oh?" Ponky Larreighffriebollaux sounded perplexed. He very rarely dealt with things that weren't real.

"It's one of those things that the beak who taught us English at Eton was always cluntering on about. A meta . . . meta-something . . . ?"

"Metronome?" Ponky offered helpfully.

"No, I don't think it was that."

"Meteor? Metropolis?"

Blotto shook his head. "No, those both miss the bull. Oh . . ." His brow furrowed in frustration. "Can't remember the exact word, but it starts with 'meta' and then has a number after it."

"'Meta-five'," Ponky suggested.

"No." Then it came to Blotto, like a lightning bolt slicing through ice cream. "'Meta-four'!" he announced triumphantly. "And basically, what it means is that . . . all right, there isn't actually a cloud over the sun, but it *feels* like there's a cloud over the sun."

Ponky looked puzzled. This wasn't difficult for him. His fall-back expression had always been one of puzzlement. But he was feeling even more puzzled than usual. Blotto's words were leading him into deep and unmapped waters of speculation.

"And we're still not talking about a *real* sun or a *real* cloud?"

"No."

"So, you're saying", Ponky suggested tentatively, "that, though it's a lovely day, you're tasting a bit of crud in the crumpet . . . ?"

"You're bong on the nose there, Ponky me old trouserpress! And for me the crud in this particular crumpet is knowing that this is the last cricket match of the season. All right, fair biddles, soon it'll be the

4

hunting season, and there's nothing I like better than sitting astride my hunter Mephistopheles and blowing the wind up a fox . . . but I still . . ." he concluded wistfully, "I still miss my cricket in the winter."

"Yes, with you all the way up the avenue," Ponky agreed. "But you know, Blotto me old sock-suspender, there are other parts of the world where cricket matches happen all year round."

"Oh, I know that," said Blotto dismissively, "but they're all spoffing foreign places where they don't speak English. India . . . Australia . . ."

"I think they do speak English in Australia."

"Not *proper* English."

"No," Ponky agreed. "Not proper English. On the other hand," he went on, "they do play cricket in America."

"No, they don't. They play baseball, which is a game where nothing happens and the whole rombooley goes on for hours and hours. Totally unlike cricket."

Ponky Larreighffriebollaux held up a hand to stem his friend's flow. "There is a place in the United States where they play proper cricket."

"Oh yes? And I'm the Emperor of Japan," said a sceptical Blotto. "So where is this imaginary place?"

"Hollywood," Ponky replied. "There's a community of English actors out there who play proper cricket."

"Do they, by Wilberforce?"

"And what is more, I've just received an invitation to make up a scratch team of Peripherals to participate in a few matches out there next month."

"Really?" asked Blotto, his voice thick with excitement. "In the winter?"

"You've potted the black there. So," Ponky took pity on the yearning expression on his friend's face, "Blotto me old boot-scraper, how do you fancy joining the Peripherals for a short winter tour of Hollywood?"

Devereux Lyminster looked as though all his birthdays had come at once. And it wasn't only the thought of continuing to play cricket through the winter that boosted his emotional barometer. He liked the movies, particularly ones involving cowboys. And of those his favourites featured a hero called Chaps Chapple, played by a big hunk of an actor called Hank Urchief.

Whatever gluepot his dastardly enemies forced him into, Chaps could always find a way out of it. He would defy horrendous odds in battles with the local Apaches and always somehow come out on top. He wore a leather waistcoat and the leather chaps that provided his nickname, and his handsome face was shaded by a broad-brimmed leather hat. He rode a horse called Lightning, who was completely white (the choice of horse colours in black and white movies being naturally limited). Chaps had a sidekick called Tubby, who was a deaf-mute. (This was actually a difficult concept to get across in a silent movie, so there were many captions reminding the audience of Tubby's deaf-muteness.)

Blotto, far too diffident and English to recognise any heroic qualities in himself, worshipped Chaps Chapple as a hero from a distance.

6

A particular favourite movie was one called *Chaps' Lonesome Stand*, which he must have watched a dozen times.

In it a beautiful innocent young woman has been kidnapped by the notorious O'Connor Gang and taken away to their mountain hideout. (There was always a beautiful innocent young woman in a Chaps Chapple movie. She loved him and he had feelings for her too, but he could never settle down because he was too busy being a hero. Besides, their parting at the end meant that another beautiful innocent young actress could be cast in the next movie.) Chaps sets out to rescue her with his trusty sidekick Tubby.

Unfortunately, as soon as they arrive at the O'Connors' hideout, there's a shoot-out, during which the firing mechanism of Chaps Chapple's rifle is shot away by one bullet, while another immobilises Tubby by hitting him in the shoulder (always the favoured destination for a nonfatal wound in the land of cinema).

So Chaps Chapple has to complete the rescue on his own, armed with a rifle, which is now only of use as a club, and facing the firepower of a dozen heavily armed O'Connor desperados.

Which of course he does by a variety of daring stratagems. One of the last is releasing a pile of barrels to knock down most of the O'Connor gang. Then Chaps Chapple leaps up to the beam, which supports lifting gear on the side of a building, grabs hold of the rope and, holding his useless rifle in front of him, swings down in an arc, sending the remaining villains scattering in disarray.

In this way, he saves both the beautiful innocent young girl and his wounded sidekick. Tubby is taken to the local doctor to be patched up, while the girl mimes the caption: "I WISH YOU COULD STAY AWHILE, MISTER." Chaps Chapple shakes his head and his caption reads: "SORRY, MA'AM. I CAN'T STAY AROUND WHILE THERE'S STILL VILLAINS OUT THERE WHOSE EVIL PLANS MUST BE FOILED." Then, after touching the brim of his leather hat to the lady, he rides off into the sunset.

But it wasn't just the possibility of meeting the human embodiment of Chaps Chapple, Hank Urchief, that made Hollywood attractive to Blotto. The place exercised another, more personal, magnetism for him.

In the South of France some years earlier, he had met and taken rather a shine to a silent film actress called Mimsy La Pim. She was very beautiful and there was intellectual compatibility between them (in other words, they shared exactly the same level of brainpower).

There had even been some discussion of marriage, which continued until both became aware of the great gulf between them. It wasn't a class thing. Even though Devereux Lyminster was the scion of a noble British family who could trace their ancestry back to the Norman Conquest, while Mimsy La Pim had been born Pookie Klunch to dirt-poor (and dirt-covered) farmers in Idaho, Blotto still believed that love could bridge the gap. It was only when Mimsy La Pim told him that she wanted to continue her career in Hollywood that he realised his hopes of marriage were doomed. It wasn't the thought of her working as an actress that broke the deal, it was the idea of the wife of someone of Blotto's breeding working at *anything* that put the kibosh on it. Reluctantly, therefore, they parted company in the South of France, sadly agreeing that they would never meet again.

But that didn't mean that Blotto stopped *seeing* her, though. Every time the *Tawcestershire Echo* announced a new movie starring Mimsy La Pim, he would be occupying the best seat in Tawsford Picture Palace on its first showing. And while he watched her as the innocent prey of dastardly villains, while he saw her once again being released from the bonds that tied her to the tracks just before the train bisected her, Blotto dreamed of what might have been.

He remembered her beauty, the helmet of black hair, the lips, grey in the movies but a vivid scarlet in the flesh. Mimsy La Pim . . .

And now he was actually on his way to join the world in which she lived and worked. He no longer entertained thoughts of marriage, but the more he listened to other boddoes talking, the more he realised that the context of marriage was not the only way in which it was possible to spend time with members of the gentler sex. Rather slowly, Blotto was catching up with the laxness of contemporary standards of morality.

Was it possible that he might meet Mimsy La Pim again in Hollywood?

CHAPTER
TWO

A Meeting With the Mater

There are ice-covered rocky outcrops in the Himalayas more welcoming than the face of the Dowager Duchess of Tawcester. Blotto and his uncannily beautiful and brilliant sister Twinks had grown up with no expectation of tenderness from their mother and their lack of hope in that department had proved amply justified.

Though she had on occasion been known to show affection for puppies or foals, it was not an indulgence she thought should be squandered on her children. It would only weaken them, rendering them unequal to the challenges that life would inevitably throw their way. The ancestral glue that held together families like the Lyminsters had always been duty rather than love.

This did not cause any resentment. Blotto and Twinks would have found it odd — and rather uncomfortable — had their mother ever expressed any tenderness towards them. There was nothing soft about the British aristocracy. They remained as cranky and unforgiving as the Tawcester Towers plumbing.

The Dowager Duchess had summoned her two younger offspring to the Blue Morning Room, which was where she always held court, and from where she ran the affairs of Tawcester Towers. While her husband had been alive, she had taken all decisions that concerned the estate, and she did not let his death and the succession of their son to the ducal title change that. Whatever happened at Tawcester Towers was decided by the Dowager Duchess.

Her older son, the current Duke, was believed to be somewhere on the premises that day. The estates were so large that family members were quite used to not encountering each other for months on end. Indeed, the Dowager Duchess's late husband always had to be reintroduced to his offspring on the rare occasions when they met.

So that morning the current Duke (universally known as Loofah) was probably hiding in one of the mansion's many rooms. When in residence at Tawcester Towers, he spent as much time as possible out shooting and, if he had to be inside the house, trying to avoid his wife (universally known as Sloggo) and their large number of daughters (which were all her busy womb seemed able to produce). The demand for a male heir in a family like the Lyminsters was unremitting, however, and though the Duke of Tawcester didn't know much in the great scheme of things, he did know where his duty lay. As a result, he stuck to the grim task of trying to impregnate his wife with something that wouldn't wear dresses when it grew up. So far, though, without success.

The Duke rarely visited the Blue Morning Room, but Blotto and Twinks had been in awe of the place since their nursery days. A summons there from the Dowager Duchess rarely boded well for either of them and, though both now in their twenties, they still approached the place as errant schoolboys might their headmaster's study.

"But you've already been to America," was their mother's comment when the proposed Hollywood jaunt had been explained to her. "There might be a possible excuse for visiting a foreign country once, but to do so a second time smacks of masochism. Not to say a lack of appropriate patriotic feeling."

"But, Mater," objected Blotto, "I will be being as patriotic as a spoffing red, white and blue bulldog. Can there be anything in the world more patriotic than taking the values of cricket to savage lands?"

"Hm," said the Dowager Duchess.

The fact that her response was ambivalent rather than downright condemnatory encouraged Blotto to pursue his argument. "I mean, get those old American pineapples up to snuff with the rules of cricket and they'll probably be a bit quicker out of the traps joining in wars and things."

The Dowager Duchess looked sternly unconvinced by this suggestion. But then the silvery voice of Twinks joined the conversation.

Twinks, it should be reiterated, was a young woman of extraordinary beauty. She had an exquisite figure, silken blonde hair, porcelain skin and eyes that were not so much blue as azure. Every man she met fell for her, like a Douglas Fir assailed by lumberjacks. Twinks rarely felt capable of reciprocating the adoration of these amorous swains — she regarded them as an irritation on the scale of midges beside a Scottish loch — but she was far too well brought up to make her rejections anything less than gracious.

If beauty was all she brought to the table, Twinks would still have been engraved on the memory of all who encountered her, but she also had brains. Within that delicate cranium there operated a calculating machine of unrivalled proficiency. If there is a God who allocates brainpower, then He'd granted Twinks the thinking capacity of at least a dozen ordinary humans. And though He was correspondingly ungenerous to Blotto, this couldn't have mattered less. Twinks had brains enough, and to spare, for the both of them. Her brother had never questioned or resented her intellectual superiority. He just knew that if Twinks had an idea, it was bound to be a buzzbanger.

And that day in the Blue Morning Room Twinks did have an idea to suggest to the Dowager Duchess. She knew there were three subjects bound immediately to engage her mother's attention — dogs, horses and the one she was about to raise, the state of the Tawcester Towers plumbing.

The system was antiquated and, in spite of attempts at renovation, no improvements seemed to bring a lasting solution to the problems. It still clattered and clanked throughout the night, sounding as though ghostly armies had been woken from their deep enchanted sleep to do battle. And in the furthest bathrooms of the building the taps still failed to produce more than a trickle of cold brown water.

Maintaining the Tawcester Towers plumbing wolfed down money at a rate that made the cost of keeping racehorses in training look like a bargain.

On more than one occasion Blotto and Twinks had brought back from their adventures large amounts of the old jingle-jangle, sometimes in the form of gold ingots, but the estate's renewed solvency never lasted long. However much cash was poured into the ravenous maw of the Tawcester Towers plumbing, the creature remained insatiable, growling out a sequence of clanks that translated as, "Feed me! Feed me!"

So when, that day in the Blue Morning Room, Twinks mentioned the subject, she knew she would command her mother's full attention. "Mater," she trilled, "I was just having a little cogitette about the Tawcester Towers plumbing."

Two stern, unyielding eyes focused on her through their rockery of wrinkles. "What about it?" demanded the Dowager Duchess.

"I gather we're once again in something of a swamphole over finances."

"We always are," said her mother tersely.

"Well, I've thought of a way out of this particular clammy corner."

"Oh?"

"I was thinking it would be a beezer wheeze for me to go to America with Blotto."

"It has not yet been agreed", the Dowager Duchess boomed, "that Blotto is going to America. And I can certainly think of no reason why you should go with him."

"The Tawcester Towers plumbing, Mater — that's the reason."

"Explain that most unlikely assertion. We have a perfectly adequate plumber in Tawsford town. The only thing wrong with him is his bourgeois insistence on being paid for his services, a tendency which I discover is becoming all too prevalent among tradespersons. To travel to America in search of a better plumber seems to me a ridiculous extravagance."

"No, Mater, you've got the wrong end of the treacle spoon. I wasn't suggesting going to America for a plumber. That would be a pure waste of gingerbread. No, what I had in mind was going to America to find a husband."

"Ah." This did not seem to the Dowager Duchess such a crazy idea. "Do you have anyone in mind for this role?"

"No, not at this precise mo, but America — and Hollywood in particular — is packed to the gunwales with rich husband material."

"Yes . . ." the craggy old woman mused portentously. "I seem to remember we tried something similar with Blotto. He was going to be married to Mary Chapstick, daughter of Luther P. Chapstick III."

"But that wheeze rather hit the buffers," said Blotto, colouring slightly at the recollection of his embarrassment at the time.

The Dowager Duchess was still musing. "Of course, a lot of young men of our breeding — well, not quite of ours obviously, but *aspiring* to our breeding — have balanced the family finances by marrying American

15

gels, but I don't think it's happened too much with our gels marrying American men."

"Well, that could all change," said Twinks. "If I go out with Blotto to the jolly old US of A, then I'm bound to meet some Hollywood tycoon or Texas oil millionaire with spondulicks spilling out of his lugs. Then I twiddle up the old reef knot with him and — sparksissimo — problemo solvo!"

This prompted another "Hm" from the Dowager Duchess. While the prospect of her younger son being married off to a rich American and never returning to Tawcester Towers had caused her no qualms, the thought of her daughter doing the same thing was not quite so appealing. Not for sentimental reasons, of course. It was just that she had plans to breed from Twinks. Line her up with some suitable Duke and the Lyminster dynasty could be considerably strengthened.

On the other hand, all of that would take time. Any dealings with the British aristocracy took time — not only blue blood but lethargy too ran through their veins. And the Tawcester Towers plumbing, like time and tide, waited for no man. Only that morning the butler Grimshaw had brought news of a burst pipe having drenched an under-housemaid in her bed. Normally such a domestic accident to one of her inferiors would have been of no interest to the Dowager Duchess but, as Grimshaw pointed out, since all the servants' rooms were in the poky attics on the top floor, it was only a matter of time before water seeped through into the rest of the house.

Something needed to be done about the Tawcester Towers plumbing.

When the Dowager Duchess made decisions, she did so quickly. "Very well, Twinks," she said. "Go to America and don't bother to come back until you've got a very rich husband."

"Tickey-tockey, Mater. There's got to be a Texas oil millionaire with my name engraved on him out there somewhere."

"In fact, you needn't bother to come back at all, so long as the money crosses the Atlantic."

"I'll sort it out as quick as a lizard's lick."

"Good." The Dowager Duchess's beady eyes sought out the golden carriage clock on the mantelpiece. "And now I see no reason why you two should still be here. Leave me!"

"Yes, Mater," said Twinks.

"Erm . . . just one thingette . . ." said Blotto.

"What!" the Dowager Duchess turned the full power of her eyebrows on to her younger son.

"Well, Mater, you've said Twinks can cross the Pond to go husband-fishing, which is all creamy éclair, but you haven't yet said whether I can go."

"Well, of course you must go!"

"Oh thanks, Mater. You see, Ponky Larreighffriebollaux is already over there — or at least he's on the boat. That's beezer, though, Mater, giving me the permish to cross the pond to play cricket."

"Not to play cricket, Blotto. Your role in going to America will be to act as chaperone to your sister."

"Good ticket," said Blotto.

As they left the Blue Morning Room, he caught the twinkle in his sibling's eye. He knew how little Twinks liked being chaperoned under any circumstances. Wherever she went, she led her own life. Which meant Blotto was going to be able to play as much cricket as he wanted in Hollywood. Hoopee-doopie!

CHAPTER
THREE

A Conference With Corky

"Into whatever hazardous situation you put yourself, milord, I regard it as my duty and honour to go with you and protect you to the last drop of my unworthy blood."

"Oh really, Corky," said Blotto, "don't talk such toffee."

He had heard many such protestations of loyalty from his chauffeur, Corky Froggett. The man, in spotless black uniform and peaked cap, stood to attention beside the equally spotless blue Lagonda. Every individual bristle of his white moustache also stood to attention.

"And to what noxious foreign hellhole are we directing ourselves this time, milord?"

"We're pootling off to the United States of America," Blotto announced.

"Oh." Corky Froggett couldn't keep a note of disappointment out of his voice. Though, like most true Englishmen, he regarded "abroad" with appropriate contempt, the chauffeur tended to grade foreign countries according to the level of animosity he was likely to encounter there. Corky's finest hour had been the war against Germany. Then he had been in his element, living in unsavoury trenches in France and only emerging to kill as many of the enemy as possible. So he didn't mind travelling to Europe, always with the secret hope that hostilities might break out again and he'd be able to continue in his God-given role as a killing machine.

But America . . . His main feeling about the place was resentment for the slowness with which they had condescended to add their strength to the Allied cause during the last little dust-up.

Still, it wouldn't do to show any reluctance to the young master, so he followed up his disappointed "Oh" with an enthusiastic "Very good, milord. And you are suggesting that I should accompany you?"

"That's the ticket, yes. It's just me going, with Twinks of course, but America's a whale of a big country and I think we'll need someone else to help with the driving."

"I will be honoured to do that, milord."

"You're a good greengage, Corky."

"Thank you, milord," said the chauffeur, recognising high praise in the young master's words.

"We sail from Liverpool on Monday, aboard the S.S. *Regal*. So I want you to ensure that you've got the Lag in zing-zing condition for then."

Corky Froggett looked slightly affronted as he tapped the car's long bonnet. "I *always* keep the Lag in zing-zing condition."

"I know you do. Sorry, shouldn't have said that — couple of toes in the mouth there."

The chauffeur looked gratified by this apology.

"You'll enjoy driving in America, Corky. Long, wide roads, though the poor saps do insist on driving the wrong side."

"Well, we could put an end to that, milord."

"Sorry, not on the same page, Corky?"

"What I'm saying, milord, is that if we insist on driving on the correct side of the road, which is of course the left, I'm sure the Yanks will quickly see the error of their ways and follow suit."

"Ye-es," said Blotto, not entirely convinced. "I think that's an experiment we might pop in the pending file."

"Very good, milord."

"Actually, Corky me old fruitbat, it's not just for your driving skills that I want you in the USA."

"Oh, milord?"

"I also want you there as a wicketkeeper." The chauffeur looked puzzled. "Oh, come on, Corky. You know that when it comes to wicketkeeping, you're the absolute panda's panties."

"I do my best, milord," came the humble response. "But there is one thing I can't help observing . . ."

"What? Come on, uncage the ferrets."

"The cricket season has ended, milord."

"Ah, now this is where everything's pure strawberry jam with dollops of cream. There are some Americans in Hollywood who play cricket *out of season!*"

"Well, I'll be . . ." When he was with the young master at such moments of surprise, Corky never finished the sentence. Such language might be acceptable below stairs but it was not appropriate in the company of aristocrats.

"And that is the reason why you are making this trip to the USA, is it, milord?"

"Main reason, yes. Also going to see if we can find some pot-brained pineapple rich enough to marry Twinks."

"Very good, milord. One other thing . . ."

"What's that?"

Corky Froggett looked at the Lagonda by his side. "The last time you went to America, milord, you came back with a secret compartment fitted to the underside of this car."

"You're bong on the nose there, Corky. We gotten it done by some stenchers in the Mafia."

"I beg your pardon, milord?"

"What is it, Corky?"

"I don't understand, milord, what you mean by 'We gotten it done'."

"Ah well, you see, I'm kind of doing a bit of prep for pongling off to the States. Americans do say 'gotten' quite a lot."

"Do they, milord? When?"

"That's the tick in the teacup, Corky. I'm not quite sure when they *do* say it. So I thought if I practised putting the occasional 'gotten' into my conversation, I might be doing it naturally by the time I get there."

"I understand completely, milord."

"Beezer! You've gotten it in one. Give that pony a rosette!"

"Thank you, milord. Going back to the compartment beneath the Lagonda . . ."

"Good ticket, Corky, yes."

"Well, I was wondering, milord, whether you wished me to remove it before we take her on the S.S. *Regal* on Monday."

Blotto's brow furrowed beneath its thatch of hair. But his indecision only lasted a moment. The furrows smoothed themselves out as he announced, "Leave it there, Corky. You never know when you're going to need somewhere secret to hide a load of bullion, say . . . or a dead body."

"Very good, milord," said Corky Froggett.

A couple of days before they were due to leave, Blotto found himself in London with some time to kill. Twinks had wanted to sharpen up her wardrobe for the American trip and that involved visiting a series of exclusive shops in Mayfair. Blotto had been happy to drive her up in the Lagonda, but shopping wasn't really his length of banana, so they agreed to separate and meet up three hours later in the bar of The Dorchester.

Blotto took the opportunity to have a very good lunch at one of his clubs and, while he was wandering back to where he'd parked the Lagonda, he passed a toyshop and noticed that one of the display windows was full of jumping frogs.

Now normally Blotto didn't have strong feelings about frogs. His outlook on the natural world was benign. He bore no ill will towards animals. He certainly bore no ill will to the ones he shot in such large numbers. It was nothing personal, just the way he'd been brought up.

But the jumping frogs in the toyshop window struck a new chord in him. They looked such jolly fun, he wanted to own one.

Inside the shop an unctuous assistant demonstrated the toy. It was powered by clockwork. Wind the thing up and you got a full minute of jumping around.

What was more, once inside the shop, Blotto was even more fascinated to discover that the frog croaked as well as jumped.

The purchase was instantly made. As the assistant wrapped the toy up in its box, he asked, "Well, sir, I'm sure that when this is unwrapped in front of the Christmas tree, it's destined to make some lucky child very happy."

"No," said Blotto. "It's for me."

CHAPTER
FOUR

Crossing the Pond

The journey across the Atlantic on the S.S. *Regal* was predictable. All the unattached young men — and a good few of the attached ones — fell in love with Twinks. And all the unattached young women — and a good few of the attached, particularly the older ones — fell in love with Blotto.

The siblings reacted to these attentions in their characteristic but contrasting manners. Twinks maintained her usual midge-swatting insouciance, whereas Blotto remained totally unaware of the stirrings he engendered in female bosoms and did nothing. But the way he did nothing only made the women even more in love with him.

Brother and sister passed their time on shipboard in ways that suited them. Apart from spending quite a lot of time in his state room playing with his clockwork jumping frog, Blotto got enough young men together to play some entertaining deck cricket matches. And Twinks found in the liner's library a copy of Sun Tzu's *The Art of War* in the original Chinese from the fifth century BC. It seemed obvious to her to fill her daylight hours by translating it into Gujarati.

For the duration of the crossing, Corky Froggett didn't leave the ship's hold. This was partly in order to keep an eye on — and keep highly polished — the precious Lagonda, which had been lashed into position with strong ropes. On the same level as the hold was the accommodation for the ship's crew and servants — "below stairs" translated to "below decks" — and it was here that Corky made the acquaintance of one of the waitresses who worked in the First Class dining room. Since she was impressed by his military bearing and of a giving disposition, he passed many pleasant hours in her cabin, enjoying not only her ample charms but also a variety of delicious gourmet dishes she purloined from her place of employment. So despite the fact that he never saw daylight, Corky Froggett's first experience of transatlantic travel was a very pleasant one.

Because she was so caught up in her translation, Twinks spent most of her time in her state room, only emerging in the evenings to join cocktail parties and have dinner in the First Class dining room. There she was invariably seated at the Captain's table, and usually next to the Captain (he being another of the amorous swains who'd fallen for her like a midshipman plummeting from a crow's nest).

He was a man of considerable charm and suavity, but once Twinks had established that he didn't have enough money to be the saviour of Tawcester Towers' plumbing, she lost interest in him.

There was, however, another guest at the Captain's table on the second evening of their voyage who seemed promising, at least from a financial point of view. He was seated next to Twinks on the other side of the Captain, and was tall and thin with a Latinate look about him. His skin was deep brown and his dark eyes twinkled like rogue olives. His centre-parted black hair was slicked down so firmly it looked almost as if it had been painted on. He was unquestionably handsome and caused even more fluttering in the dovecotes of the female passengers than Blotto.

The reason was that the man was not only handsome, he was also well known and fabulously wealthy. His was a face recognised in every part of the world that had been reached by Hollywood movies, as he was Toni Frangipani, the star of numerous silent films. He had played more lovers than Catherine the Great got through, so as a fantasy, he inhabited the dreams of millions of women.

And it was clear from his first words to Twinks that he was well aware of his magnetism. "Tonighta you are the lucky one," he said in a voice that was as squeaky as an unoiled hinge.

"Sorry, not on the same page?" said Twinks.

"You are the lucky one who issa sitting next to me."

"Don't talk such toffee," she said coolly. When it came to *froideur*, Twinks was her mother's daughter. "You're the lucky one who's sitting next to *me*."

He turned on her the smouldering eyes which had ignited answering fires in so many ardent female fans. He seemed to be taking her in for the first time. "You are notta bad looking," he said. "I havva forgotten your name."

As it was only moments since they had been introduced by the Captain, Twinks found this downright insulting. "I am Honoria Lyminster," she announced in full Dowager Duchess mode. "Also known as Twinks."

"So whatta do I call you?"

"You can call me milady," came the frosty response. "And who are you?"

Of course, she knew perfectly well who he was, but she didn't think he should assume that she did. Though the most tolerant and modern of young women, Twinks still retained her values when it came to the business of fame. If you were a member of the British aristocracy, then the whole concept of it was rather degrading. People of her class should not have to tell people who they were; the lower orders should just *know*. The pursuit of fame was frankly vulgar. It reeked of that most awful of crimes in the British upper class pantheon, showing off — something at which foreigners, particularly Americans, indulged in far too often, in Twinks's view.

The idea that the fame of some jumped-up actor should be mentioned in the same breath as the celebrity of a family like the Lyminsters, whose roots went back to the Norman Conquest, was simply ludicrous.

"My name issa Toni Frangipani." The words came out clumsily as it was many years since he had had to use them, many years since he had met anyone who did not recognise him.

"And what do you do?"

"I am a filma star. I am the most famousa filma star in the worlda."

"Oh, really?" said Twinks drily.

"I am also the most handsoma man in the worlda."

"In whose opinion?"

"In the opinion of every reader of every filma magazine in the worlda."

"Well, that hardly wins the coconut," said Twinks.

"You do notta understand. There are millions offa women who would givva alla that they possessa to be sitting where you are tonight."

Twinks's azure eyes scanned the room. "Well, maybe you should find one of the poor deluded darlings. I'd be more than happy to park my chassis somewhere else."

The black eyes glinted, the perfect Roman brow corrugated. Toni Frangipani was in uncharted territory. No woman had ever before reacted to him in this way. His perplexity quickly translated into a determination to keep his dinner companion with him at all costs.

"Would you like a signeda photographa offa me?" he asked. This generous offer had never before been refused.

Twinks's elegant eyebrows arched. "What for? I know what you look like. A photograph would be about as much use to me as a tail-curler to a Manx cat."

"It issa facta", said Toni Frangipani, "that wherever I staya in the worlda I have to keepa my bedroom doora locked."

"Why? Are you a somnambulist?"

"Whatta?"

"A boddo who walks in their sleep. Are you saying you have to keep your bedroom locked so you don't start pongling around on the landing in the middle of the night?"

The film star was deeply affronted. "Noa. It is notta to keep me fromma leaving my bedda room. It is to keepa people from coming into my bedda room."

"Oh," said Twinks without interest.

"And when I saya 'people', of coursa what I mean issa 'women'. Alla women want to be in my bedda room."

"Not all," said Twinks.

At another table, another, more charming charm offensive was being unleashed. Blotto had been seated next to a lady of maturely leggy charms. Her dark hair was cut in a fashionable bob, her hazel eyes sparkled under perfectly arched eyebrows and her full lips were outlined in startling scarlet. The colour was picked up in the silk of her dress. She was, in fact, some twenty years older than her dinner companion, but the artistry of her make-up halved that number.

Her accent was basically English, with just an edge of American on certain words. She was an actress named Zelda Finch, convent-educated in genteel Virginia Water, who in her twenties had been the toast of London's West End. Lured across to Hollywood, she'd made a considerable name for herself playing woman-in-jeopardy roles. If a director wanted threatened innocence in his next movie, then Zelda Finch was the go-to actress for the part. She'd lost count of the number of times she had been rescued from a burning house, had her hand grasped just as she was about to fall off a precipice or been tied down to railway lines by a dastardly villain with a fully twirled moustache. She was the mistress of wide-eyed horror and loving reconciliation.

The innocence so prized in Zelda Finch's screen performances was, however, not reflected in her private life. She was known in Hollywood as "The Odds" because she'd been laid so often, and her affairs kept the film community's gossip columnists like Heddan Schoulders constantly supplied with new material.

However, as her fortieth birthday approached — though in all publicity material she was said to be ten years younger — Zelda Finch decided a change of lifestyle was needed. Her agent seemed to be calling less often with new offers for her to be tied to railway lines. She knew there was a whole generation of younger actresses whose innocence and jeopardy were more appealing to the studio moguls and their eager audiences. She was also aware that the kind of lovers she attracted were no longer from the "A-list" — indeed they were slipping ever further down the alphabet — so she decided she needed the safety of marriage.

Not just safety, but also financial security. Since most of the major studio bosses were currently supplied with their latest wives (as well as the requisite number of mistresses), and since Zelda had sufficient self-knowledge to recognise how unreliable actors were, she had turned her eye towards the ranks of directors.

From them she selected the biggest beast of the lot: Gottfried von Klappentrappen, the king of the Hollywood spectacular. His movies were more extravagant than anyone else's. No one created more epic historical panoramas. No one employed more thousands of extras. No one had a worse reputation as a screaming fascist on set. And no one made more money from the international distribution of his films. Nor indeed had many men been through as many divorces as Gottfried von Klappentrappen.

Having identified her quarry, Zelda Finch went into active planning mode. She caught the director on the rebound, still smarting from his sixth broken marriage. All his previous wives had been beautiful actresses. Gottfried von Klappentrappen was living proof that what made a man attractive to the opposite sex was not looks — in his case a body with the contours of a tennis ball and a face like a boiled prawn — but what he had in his wallet.

Once Zelda had decided it was her turn to share its contents, she moved quickly. It wasn't difficult to make the acquaintance of her target. Everyone went to the same Hollywood parties, and it required only a few well-directed compliments to von Klappentrappen's masculinity to secure an invitation for a dinner à *deux*. Zelda knew that if she could get him into bed, the deal was done. Her experience and sexual athleticism were such that she felt any man who had tasted the delights of her body would be left wanting more.

So it proved with Gottfried von Klappentrappen. Though she didn't rate his prowess highly compared to her previous list of lovers, she persevered. Zelda had always thought of sex as a means to an end, and in her current pursuit the end was marriage to von Klappentrappen.

He, however, after the discomforts and costs generated by his previous wives, was in no hurry to take on another. The new status quo, having Zelda as a skilled and acquiescent lover with whom he assiduously avoided being seen in public, suited him very well and enabled him to concentrate totally on the new silent epic he was directing for Humungous Studios, *The Trojan Horse*.

But Zelda was not to be defeated. She took affairs into her own hands and contacted Hollywood's premier gossip columnist, the aforementioned Heddan Schoulders. The story she confided was translated and published in Heddan's inimitable style.

Hot news! No secrets in Hollywood, we all know that. So it was bound to come out soon that jodhpured movie supremo Gottfried von Klappentrappen has just taken another trip down the aisle. Seventh time lucky, let's hope, Gottie! And the latest Frau von Klappentrappen is British-born vamperoonie Zelda Finch. She's managed to tame a good few Hollywood hunks in her time, so who'll be holding the riding crop in that household? Gottie, incidentally, if asked about it, will deny that the marriage has taken place and change the subject to his new Humungous Studios boomeroonie *The Trojan Horse*. You can hide a lotta soldiers in one of those, Gottie, but you can't hide a secret marriage in Hollywood! As ever, you heard it here first from your close lady-buddy Heddan Schoulders, who's got her ear to more grounds than a coffee percolator.

It worked. Gottfried von Klappentrappen got so sick of being congratulated on his secret wedding to Zelda Finch that he organised a secret wedding to Zelda Finch. He also cast her as Medusa in *The Trojan Horse*. So, not for the first time, Zelda got what she wanted.

Not all that she wanted, though. Her new husband was, in her category of lovers, a "bib" (i.e., "boring in bed"). So Zelda had to make alternative arrangements, which included travelling to England for the purpose, so she told her husband, of visiting her ailing mother (dead now for fourteen years), but actually to visit a series of ex-lovers.

Rather than satisfying her, though, these encounters only served to sharpen her appetite. So she was still on the lookout on the S.S. *Regal*, which to her mind made it serendipitous that she was seated next to Blotto at dinner.

"You're English," observed Zelda Finch, starting the conversation in an uncontroversial manner.

"I certainly am, by Wilberforce," Blotto responded.

"Me too."

"It's the only thing to be." He looked around the multiple-chandeliered dining room. "One can only feel sorry for the poor thimbles who got the wrong end of the sink plunger by being born in foreign places. Tough Gorgonzola for them, eh? That kind of misfortune could take the icing off the Swiss bun for the rest of your life."

"Probably," Zelda conceded. "Why are you called Blotto?"

His brow beneath its thatch of golden hair crinkled. He had been brought up in the kind of family where nicknames didn't mean anything, you were just given one. "Because I am," he replied.

"I'm an actress in the movies." Zelda waited for Blotto to say that of course he knew who she was, that her face was famous around the world.

But he didn't. Instead he said, "I met an actress in the movies once." A dreaminess came into his blue eyes.

"Oh? Who was she?"

"Mimsy La Pim."

"Really?" Zelda's lips pursed into the mouth of a much older woman. She recognised the name. Mimsy was one of that generation of younger actors who were getting asked to play the parts of innocents being tied to railway lines that she used to be offered. She moved the conversation quickly on. "Are you married, Blotto?"

"Great whiffling water rats, no!"

"Not for lack of opportunity, I would imagine."

His puzzlement returned. "Sorry, not on the same page . . .?"

"I mean that I'm sure there are plenty of young ladies who would be ecstatic to be married to you."

Blotto's handsome face purpled. "Don't talk such meringue."

Zelda had been too frequently caught out in Hollywood by men who turned out to be "not the marrying kind" that she asked, "But you think you will get married one day?"

"'Fraid so," he replied gloomily. "I've had a clear round so far, but it can't last. One day the Mater will summon me to the Blue Morning Room in Tawcester Towers — that's where we hang up our jim-jams, actually — and tell me who I'm going to twiddle the old reef knot with."

"But until that dread moment you are footloose and fancy-free?" Zelda Finch always liked to check out the ground before embarking on one of her amours. She had no moral objection to consorting with married men, but she knew wives could be a pain, behaving as if they had some sort of exclusive rights over the spouse in question. So it was a minor relief when Blotto confirmed that he had no ongoing attachments.

"After dinner," said Zelda, her voice sinking to a new level of sultriness, "there's something I'd like to show you in my state room."

"Really?" Blotto was intrigued.

"Oh yes," she murmured thrillingly. "There's a game we can play which I know you'll enjoy."

"Toad in the hole!" said Blotto. "You don't mean you've got an indoor cricket set?"

CHAPTER
FIVE

State Room Keys

It was a new experience for Toni Frangipani, talking to Twinks. Since his teens back in Sicily, every woman he'd met had instantly rolled over like a kitten to have her tummy tickled, but this one seemed immune to his charms. And her behaviour produced an unusual reaction in him. The more Twinks put him down, the less she appeared to be impressed by him, the more determined he was that she should succumb. She had become a challenge for him.

His usual approach to women didn't require much effort. All he had to do was just smoulder quietly and they offered themselves to him. With Twinks, though, he found he was having to use his charm. It was a weapon in his armoury that hadn't been deployed much, particularly since the movies had made him world famous, so he wasn't very skilled in using it.

The only responses his stumbling compliments elicited were yawns and admonitions not to talk such toffee. And the way Twinks kept reaching into her sequined reticule to consult her jewel-encrusted pocket watch was hardly encouraging. The last mouthful of dinner clearly couldn't come soon enough for her.

The food was, of course, wonderful. First Class dining on S.S. *Regal* was created by some of the foremost chefs from both sides of the Atlantic, though most of the passengers were so inured to gourmet meals that they hardly noticed what they were eating. That evening the menu had started with a chilled consommé of partridge, followed by sole meunière, and then mutton in caper sauce, all interspersed with a profusion of entremets and sorbets. Champagne and other vintage wines flowed like Niagara. Next came a delicate four-cheese soufflé, followed by that popular concoction of strawberries, meringue and cream known as Eton Mess. This last was presented in vast cut-glass vessels, from which the waiters served portions to the preoccupied guests.

When the Eton Mess arrived Toni Frangipani was made forcibly aware of the fact that Twinks would soon be leaving, so he resorted to a final tactic that he rarely needed to use. Reaching into his waistcoat pocket he produced a key, which he handed to her.

"Thissa," he said, "is the spara key to mya state rooma. Numero uno. I willa see you there."

"No, you willa not!" Twinks announced with an unarguable finality.

And as she left the First Class dining room, she hurled the key into the nearest large cut-glass container of Eton Mess, where it sank through the layers of fruit meringue and cream.

Twinks's gesture did not go unnoticed by the other guests, and a ripple of giggling accompanied her departure. The brow of Toni Frangipani, who was not used to being laughed at, looked like thunder.

But Twinks did not notice that.

Nor did she notice the unfriendly looks of two bulky Mediterranean types at a side table, who had been watching her and Toni Frangipani all evening.

Which meant she also missed the throat-cutting gesture that Toni directed, with a nod towards her, at the two men.

And she was completely unaware that the hoodlums were working for the Mafia boss, Lenny "The Skull" Orvieto.

Blotto felt the key in the trouser pocket of his dinner suit and remembered Zelda Finch's instructions to him. "Wait half an hour after everyone has left the dining room, then come to my state room. Number two. Let yourself in and then our little game can start."

He had responded with an enthusiastic "Tickey-tockey!" Of course, he reminded himself, Zelda was English. That explained everything. Only an English-woman would have thought to bring an indoor cricket set on to a transatlantic liner. Great Wilberforce, he thought, not for the first time, it's really sad how much foreign people miss just by being foreign.

He reached into his other trouser pocket and felt the reassuring outline of his clockwork jumping frog. When Zelda wanted a break from cricket, he could show her some of its tricks.

Blotto checked his new-fangled wristwatch. It was time. Half an hour had elapsed since that last guest had left the dining room. He made his way towards state room number two.

Another visitor in the same circumstances might have moved surreptitiously, might have checked to see if there was anyone around, might have waited until the coast was clear before letting himself into the state room. No such thought occurred to Blotto. This was partly due to the fact that very few thoughts ever occurred to him, but also because his mind was devoid of any trace of guilt about what he was doing.

So he failed to notice that his use of the key to enter state room number two was observed by the two heavy-set Mediterraneans who had watched his sister so closely at dinner and who were now standing guard outside number one. Nor did Blotto notice the grim looks of complicity that Lenny "The Skull" Orvieto's men exchanged after he disappeared into Zelda Finch's room.

She had changed out of her scarlet dress into a silken negligée. Though it was full length, the material was so diaphanous that her every contour was visible. And, it has to be said, excellent contours she had, all of which were displayed to advantage as she lolled lasciviously on a chaise longue.

"Blotto," she trilled, "welcome to my world."

"Good ticket," he murmured, not quite sure what response was appropriate.

"Blotto," she continued, "from the moment I first saw you this evening I was aware of an animal magnetism between us. Do you know what I mean?"

"Not really," he admitted, honest as ever. "I mean, from what I remember the beaks at Eton teaching me and my fellow muffin-eaters was that magnetism worked for metals. You know, put a chunk of metal near a magnet and they spring together like a pair of newlyweds. I hadn't got a mouse-squeak of an idea that it could work with human beings, though."

"Never mind." During dinner Zelda Finch had got the impression that Blotto was perhaps not the brightest twig on the family tree, but that didn't represent a problem. It wasn't his brains that interested her. Past experience had taught her that in such situations an excess of brains in a man was often an inconvenience. Once they started thinking about things, the outcome was generally disappointing.

"Blotto," she continued, even sultrier, "together, you and I could make sweet music."

"Ah. Sorry to put a bit of crud in that particular crumpet, but I'm afraid when it comes to music I'm an empty revolver. No control over the noises that come out of the old tooth-trap. When I join in hymns in the Tawcester Towers chapel, the village boddoes all reach for their earplugs."

"I wasn't talking literally," said Zelda.

"Good ticket," said Blotto, remembering his cricket-pitch conversation with Ponky Larreighffrieboll-aux. "You were using one of those metronome things, were you?"

Zelda Finch didn't know he meant "metaphor", but passed no comment. She simply stretched out one of her long, elegant hands towards him and said, "Touch me."

Blotto shrugged. He wasn't quite sure what game she was playing, but he reached his hand out, tapped hers and immediately withdrew it.

She let out a throaty giggle. "I meant *really* touch me."

He was once again puzzled. "I did really touch you."

"Blotto, I meant for you to touch me as only a man can touch a woman."

"Hoopee-doopee!" he murmured.

"You are all man . . ."

He concurred. "I was when I last looked."

". . . and I am all woman."

"I wouldn't argue with a lady about something like that." He still wasn't quite sure where the conversation was leading.

"And, Blotto," she panted, again reaching out towards him. "I want you to take me in your arms and lift me up to the highest point that humankind can reach."

"Beezer," said Blotto. "If that's what you want . . ."

Shortly afterwards he left the state room in a glow of satisfaction. He had done what Zelda Finch had asked him to. It had maybe been an unusual request, but he was far too much of an English gentleman to question the desires of a lady.

And it didn't occur to him to wonder how she was going to get down from the top of the wardrobe.

CHAPTER
SIX

From Sea to Shining Sea

The S.S. *Regal* docked at New York in the early evening. Although porters removed the passengers' trunks, the larger items in the hold would not be disembarked until the following day. These, of course, included the Lagonda. So while Blotto and Twinks stayed in suites at the Plaza, Corky Froggett spent the night in the car. He didn't sleep. He had heard that New York was a lawless place so he stayed awake, protecting the beloved vehicle from the attentions of the city's many hoodlums, who he expected to invade the liner's hold at any moment.

His First Class dining room waitress tried to entice him away from the car for some farewell celebrations in her cabin, but he resolutely resisted such blandishments. And when she suggested some action inside the Lagonda he was positively shocked. The thought that those sacred leather seats should be sullied by anything so vulgar was anathema to him. So the chauffeur restricted their farewells to a brief handshake and spent the night awake in the driver's seat, guarding the young master's pride and joy. That kind of loyalty to the Lyminster family was entirely characteristic of Corky Froggett.

The following morning the Lagonda was duly craned out of the hold and Corky drove it sedately to the Plaza. Though America prided itself on being the home of the automobile, the sleek lines of Blotto's car drew many admiring looks from passing New Yorkers.

Once the hotel porters had loaded the siblings' trunks and been lavishly tipped, Blotto took over the wheel and set off to drive across the United States to Hollywood. It was a long, dusty journey. However assiduously Corky Froggett cleaned and polished the Lagonda every morning, within fifteen minutes it was once again covered with dust.

Nor was the accommodation where Blotto and Twinks spent their nights up to the lavish standards of New York's Plaza. One-horse towns — and they went through a good few of them — tended to have one-horse hotels. Some were little more than grubby, dusty bedrooms on the floors above rowdy, dusty saloons. Corky Froggett, whose suspicions of the Americans did not decrease as they travelled West, spent every night on guard. He'd seen enough cowboy movies to anticipate posses of outlawed bank robbers lassoing the Lagonda, or chieftains with feathered headdresses galloping around it with blood-chilling war-cries and fusillades of burning arrows. Because he got no sleep by night, he occasionally let his guard slip sufficiently to doze during the day in the back of the Lagonda, while Blotto drove gleefully with the top down and Twinks kept commenting that everything was "Splendissimo!"

Their adventures on the journey — the dangerous shoot-outs from which Blotto rescued them, the dastardly would-be robbers fought off by Corky Froggett, the many amorous swains who fell for Twinks like giraffes on an ice rink — would provide enough material for a book. But another book, not this one you are currently reading. So, in the jargon of the movies, we will "cut to the chase" and rediscover our hero and heroine safely installed in two suites of the Hollywood Hotel on the north side of Hollywood Boulevard.

As soon as they had freshened up in their lavish bathtubs and dressed in clean clothes from their trunks (into which no speck of dust had been allowed to penetrate), Blotto and Twinks met up in one of the hotel's many bars for a leisurely drink. Though Prohibition was supposed to rule, appropriate payments to the LAPD had ensured that it was not enforced in the Hollywood Hotel. So alcohol was served without demur. Twinks ordered champagne, and Blotto was delighted to find that the barman had the skills to make his favourite cocktail, a St Louis Steamhammer.

Once the top of his cranium had settled back down after the first sip of this combustible concoction, he asked the barman to bring him a telephone. For a moment he contemplated calling Mimsy La Pim. Except, of course, he had no phone number or other contact for her.

And anyway, there were some things more important than women. He announced that he was going to call Ponky Larreighffriebollaux. "Don't want to get caught the wrong side of the calendar, Twinks me old gutbucket," he explained. "Might be a spoffing cricket match on tomorrow and it would be a shame to miss the down train. Could do with a game after all that desert-dongling."

He was quickly connected to Ponky at his hotel. "Ratteley-Baa-Baa!" said Blotto.

"Ritteley-Boo-Boo!" his friend responded. It was the form of greeting the pair always used, something that went back to their early days at Eton.

"How're you pongling, me old fruitbat?" asked Blotto.

"Knobby as a chest of drawers. And are your suspenders tight, Blotters me old shrimping net?"

"Tight as a hippo's hawser, Ponky me old boot blackener."

"Ra-ra!" said Ponky.

"Ra-ra-ra!" said Blotto.

Twinks showed no surprise at these pleasantries. She had heard them many times before, not only when her brother was speaking to Ponky Larreighffriebollaux but also to any of his other Old Etonian muffin-toasters.

"Anyway, Ponky, uncage the ferrets. Tell me the cricket forecast. Any chance of a game in the foreseeable?"

"A very good chance, Blotto. The White Knights are playing tomorrow."

"White Knights?"

"Name of the outfit I mentioned back at Tawcester Towers. Run by this actor boddo J. Winthrop Stukes. Heard of him?"

"No."

"Well, he's quite a big noise around Hollywood. An Englishman of the old school."

"Eton?"

"Yes, of course."

"Tickey-Tockey." Whenever Blotto and his associates mentioned "the old school", they always meant Eton. "So, it's White Knights v. Peripherals?"

"No, we've got our first fixture next week. Not sure who the White Knights are up against tomorrow. Bound to be some shower from the movie business."

"Good ticket. And are you padding up for the White Knights?"

"Got it in one, Blotters. Anyway, I've mentioned you to J. Winthrop, and said what a whale you are with bat and ball, and he has got a Blotto-sized hole in his team, but he won't commit himself to tattooing your name down until he's met you."

"Oh?" Blotto was slightly taken aback. "Does he know that I'm the brother of the Duke of Tawcester?"

"Oh yes."

"And that I went to Eton?"

"Oh yes."

"And he still wants to meet me to check out my credentials?"

"'Fraid he does, yes."

"Did he say why?"

"J. Winthrop Stukes says in his experience more bounders come from the aristocracy and Eton than from any other background."

Blotto nodded. "Oh well, he's got a point there, of course, yes."

J. Winthrop Stukes' mansion was in the Los Feliz area of Los Angeles, not far from Griffith Park. It was called Britannia and built in Tudor style — or at least an expensive American architect's idea of what Tudor style should be. Indeed, had Elizabeth I wanted a half-timbered residence only slightly smaller than Buckingham Palace with a private cinema, two swimming pools and garaging for a dozen cars, Britannia was pretty much what she would have come up with.

And in case any visitor hadn't yet got the message that the place was owned by an Englishman, a large union jack floated from a tall flagpole in front of the house.

Corky Froggett drove the Lagonda from the Hollywood Hotel to Britannia, diverting to pick up Ponky Larreighffriebollaux on the way. Needless to say, in the bright Californian sunshine, the car's roof was down. Ponky sat in the back with Twinks. He had first met her when she came to watch her brother excel in an Eton and Harrow match at Lord's. Predictably enough, Ponky had fallen for her like the blade of a guillotine, and his adoration had had the effect of cutting off his powers of speech. Even now, after many years of meeting her at cricket matches and other functions, he found it difficult to come up with much more than a strangled "Tiddle my pom!" by way of conversation.

So it proved that evening, while they sat side by side in the back of the Lagonda. Twinks, apparently unaware of her companion's silence, prattled on about the beauties of the Californian sunset. And Ponky Larreighffriebollaux, whose dearest dream of being so close to his idol had been realised, could only capitalise on the situation with the occasional "Tiddle my pom!"

In the trip across America Corky Froggett had become used to the perverse business of driving on the wrong side of the road, but he still didn't like it. "Surely, milord," he said as they waited outside Ponky's hotel, "we could just try driving on the left for a little while? I'm sure the Americans will soon realise it makes sense and come round to our way of thinking."

But he was due for a disappointment. The young master forbade him from making the experiment.

As the blue Lagonda crunched over the gravel towards Britannia, the vast metal-studded Tudor doors of the mansion opened and through them issued its owner.

J. Winthrop Stukes was a tall patrician figure whose eyebrows were a very good visual aid for people who might need an explanation of the expression "beetle-browed" (though there were no beetles harmed during the manufacture of his face). In spite of the Californian heat, he was dressed in a three-piece tweed suit with plus fours and thick woollen stockings. But he was far too much of a gentleman to sweat.

"Welcome to Britannia!" he boomed. He was an actor of the old school, trained by years of repertory theatre to project his voice to fill auditoria of any size.

His voice was loud enough to speak to people within a 200-yard radius without the intervention of a telephone.

Of course, this major asset — his voice — was not capitalised on when he first moved to Hollywood, because all the movies in which he appeared were silent. But now that "talkies" were beginning to be discussed, J. Winthrop Stukes anticipated a new golden age for his career. So many of the stars of silent films — like Toni Frangipani — were vocally unqualified for the rigours of talking. Foreign accents and squeaky voices didn't matter in the silent era, but the talkies would expose a whole raft of vocal inadequates. J. Winthrop Stukes gleefully relished the prospect of infinite opportunities opening up for actors with his experience.

As if rehearsing for such an eventuality, the booming tones with which he greeted Blotto, Twinks and Ponky could have been heard the other side of the Hollywood Hills.

"Excellent to see you all!" he bellowed. "A bit late for tea, but I'm sure you could manage some scones and cucumber sandwiches."

Corky Froggett was instructed to drive the Lagonda to a garage at the back of the house and go to the kitchen door, where he would be given a drink appropriate to his social status. Then Stukes led his guests through a vast hallway into an even vaster reception room, whose décor brought to mind an English gentleman's club. Shelves of leather-bound books covered the walls. Any spaces between them were filled with the mounted heads of antlered stags whose breeds were unknown in the States. There were starbursts of medieval weapons on the walls, and two suits of armour standing guard beside the main door.

Through the leaded panes of windows at the back of the house could be seen a vast expanse of flat green grass.

J. Winthrop Stukes snapped his fingers and white-jacketed servants of oriental extraction brought in tiered cake-stands loaded with sandwiches and sweet pastries. "I never think it's too late for afternoon tea," their host roared. "Though of course if you'd rather have something stronger to drink, I have a considerable supply of single malt whiskies, together with an array of gins. And, because you can't get a glass of the stuff out here that doesn't freeze your tongue off, I can offer you some specially warmed beer."

The idea was very attractive, but before giving his order, there was a point Blotto wanted to clarify. "This business of the old alkiboodles . . ." he began.

"Yes?" said Stukes. "What about it?"

"I'd heard there's some rombooley out here about booze being beyond the barbed wire. Don't you have this thing called 'Prostitution'?"

"'Prohibition'," said Twinks, helpful as ever.

"Oh yes," J. Winthrop Stukes agreed. "But we don't bother about any of that in Hollywood. We drink when we want to."

"But isn't that against the spoffing law?"

"I believe it is."

"So what do you do?" asked a very confused Blotto. "Bribe the police?"

"Yes," said Stukes blandly. "Now what would you like to drink?"

And that was the last Blotto and Twinks heard about Prohibition during their sojourn in Hollywood.

Both the male visitors, delighted to hear that such a delicacy was on offer in a backward country like America, opted for pints of warm beer. It was just like being at home. Twinks asked for a gin and orange juice.

J. Winthrop Stukes was of the opinion that everything in life should — like a game of cricket — stop for tea. In his big voice he exchanged small talk with his guests, but his small talk was inevitably about cricket, and mostly about the shortcomings of the current English national side. He proved to be very well informed on the scores of recent matches; clearly he had a very efficient communications system with the land of his birth.

Twinks, much of whose adult life had been spent listening to men talking about cricket, had mental resources to deal with the situation. While keeping a glow of interest in her azure eyes and murmuring the occasional reaction of "Splendissimo!", she mentally recited the text of her recent translation of *The Art of War* into Gujarati.

At one point J. Winthrop Stukes turned a beady eye beneath a beetle brow on Blotto and asked in a seemingly casual manner, "Do you know anything, young feller-me-lad, about the national game they play out here?"

"You mean the game the Yank boddoes play?"

"Precisely."

"It's called baseball."

"Full marks, yes. And what do you think of it?"

Another person, recently arrived in America, might have prevaricated, minced his words a little until he had sounded out his questioner's views on the subject, but it was not in Blotto's nature ever to be less than honest, so he replied, "Though I've never actually seen the game played, I gather it wouldn't be my length of banana at all. Apparently the whole clangdumble lasts for ever. People keep throwing the ball at people who keep missing it and the spectacle's about as interesting as a nun's diary."

Privately, Twinks thought that her brother's description could just as well have applied to cricket, but she was far too tactful and generous-spirited to say so.

Blotto went on, "In fact, there's not a dog's whisker of difference between baseball and an English game called 'Rounders', which is only played by girls and sissies."

There was a long silence. Then J. Winthrop Stukes rose to his feet and stretched out a hand to shake Blotto's firmly. "You're a man after my own liver, young feller-me-lad. I couldn't have described baseball better myself."

The younger man blushed his thanks.

"And in fact it was in order to put that question that I invited you over here. You see, I run this cricket team called the White Knights —"

"Yes. Ponky gave me the SP on that little caper."

53

"Tiddle my pom!" said the Ponky in question. He might have said more, but his vocabulary was, as ever, limited in the presence of Twinks.

"Anyway," Stukes went on, "it's very important that I only get the right sort of coves joining the White Knights. First of all, obviously, they have to be English. There are a few Yanks out here who don't play cricket too badly, but they can never muster the insouciance and verve of a true Brit. And they practise, which is rather unsporting and takes away the fun of the game."

"You're bong on the nose there," Blotto agreed fervently.

"Some of them, I'm sorry to say," Stukes continued, "are fans of baseball, too. In fact, some of them have even been known to see similarities between the two games."

"Well, I'll be jugged like a hare!" said Blotto, appropriately shocked.

"Tiddle my pom!" said Ponky Larreighffriebollaux, equally shocked.

"So you see, young feller-me-lad, before I offered you a game with the White Knights, it was desperately important that I found out your attitude to the game — so-called — of baseball." He snorted with blue-blooded derision. "I'm afraid my team can't carry any fellow-travellers. But I put the question to you and you came up with the perfect answer. As did Ponky when I asked him. So he'll be on the strength in the match. So, Blotto, since you've passed my test with flying colours, I'm asking if you'd be free to play for the White Knights tomorrow."

54

"Toad in the hole!" said Blotto.

"Tiddle my pom!" said Ponky.

"I've scrubbed everything else out of the diary for the next five days," said Blotto.

"Ah," said J. Winthrop Stukes. "Something I should tell you, young feller-me-lad . . . I'm afraid we don't do full five-day test matches out here."

Blotto looked as if he'd just been hit on the back of the head with a lead-filled sock (as he would be later into his Californian adventure). "That's a bit of a candle-snuffer. So what . . . do you just squeeze the whole rombooley into four days?"

"No. One day," Stukes confessed.

"Well, I'll be kippered like a herring! That's like village cricket," Blotto said contemptuously. "How in the name of Wilberforce does it work?"

"We limit the time. One side bats for three hours. Then we have lunch and the other side bats for three hours."

Blotto was so shocked by this sacrilegious abuse of his favourite game that the ability to speak deserted him for a moment. Eventually he said, "It *is* like spoffing village cricket, not like the real thing."

"We've had to do it," Stukes apologised, "because of the demands of the film industry."

And to show a bit of mercy to the spectators, thought Twinks. Though of course she would never vocalise such heresy in her brother's hearing.

"You see, young feller-me-lad, most of the chaps involved in the games are actually making movies as we speak. Some of them don't work at the weekends so we

55

have a lot of fixtures then, and if it's a weekday, one day off might be tolerated, but there's no way five would be."

"Toad in the hole!" Blotto was still in a state of shock. Typical of the Americans, he was thinking. Straightforward perversity, fiddling with something that doesn't need fiddling with and ending up spoiling it completely. Like that business of driving on the wrong side of the road. And saying "gotten" when they meant "got". Still, he was in Britannia as a guest of J. Winthrop Stukes and his breeding would not allow him to take issue with his host. He would just have to suppress his feeling of shock and move the conversation on. "So, which pineapples are we up against?" he asked. "Who's the opposition?"

"We're playing *The Trojan Horse*."

"Are we, by Denzil? Trojan, are they? I'm not sure where Trojia is."

"No, no, they're Yanks mostly. All laddies who are working out here on a movie of that name."

"*The Trojan Horse.*"

"Exactly. Gives me a bit of a problem, as it happens."

"Oh? Sorry, not on the same page?"

"Well, I'm actually in *The Trojan Horse*."

"Inside it?" The story vaguely resonated from something one of the classics beaks at Eton had talked about. "With all the soldiers?"

"No, no, no. I'm actually in the movie. Being made by Humungous Studios."

"Ah. Good ticket."

"Presumably," asked J. Winthrop Stukes with characteristic actor's vanity, "you're familiar with my screen work?"

"Screen work? What, you mean making screens like those Japanese boddoes who —?"

"No, no. My movies. Presumably you have seen all of my movies?"

"Well, er, um," said Blotto, unwilling to admit that he'd never seen any of them.

"I obviously have copies of all of them here in my private cinema," Stukes went on, "should you wish to have another viewing of some of my finest work — in fact, without sounding my own trumpet, I have to say it's some of the finest work ever seen in Hollywood — you only have to say the word."

"That's very British of you," said Blotto, "most generous." Then, quickly, before he could be dragooned into the private cinema, "And what part are you playing in *The Trojan Horse*?"

"Methuselah." Blotto had only heard of "a Methuselah" as in a very large bottle of wine, so he didn't question what a character from the Old Testament might be doing in an epic about the Trojan War. "So you see," Stukes went on, "in this forthcoming cricket match I could really be playing for either side."

"But I thought you said the White Knights were your team."

"They are."

"So you don't really have a problem, do you? A boddo's loyalty is always to his own team."

"Exactly." Stukes approved of Blotto's sentiments. The young man was clearly one of the best kind of Englishmen. If his cricket skills matched his character, he could be a very useful addition to the White Knights.

"What's this *Trojan Horse* about?" asked Blotto.

"It's about the Trojan Horse."

"Ah," said Blotto. "Good ticket."

"It's the latest epic by Gottfried von Klappentrappen."

During the encounter with Zelda Finch on the S.S. *Regal* no mention had been made of her husband, nor of the film he currently had in production, so the name rang no bells with Blotto. His sister, though, who had kept her ears open during the transatlantic crossing, took in its resonance.

J. Winthrop Stukes leant forward to his latest recruit to the White Knights and asked eagerly, "So tell me, young feller-me-lad, which side of the wicket do you bowl?"

The sun had long before sunk over the horizon of the Pacific, and it was by moonlight that the old actor led them out of the authentic Tudor French windows on to the green space at the back of Britannia. His guests realised at once that what he had built there was a full-size replica of Lord's cricket ground, complete with an exact copy of the Pavilion, containing a facsimile Long Room.

Blotto tested the ground beneath his feet. "This is tickey-tockey," he said. "Feels just like the real thing."

"So it should do, young feller-me-lad," said J. Winthrop Stukes. "Every square inch of turf on this pitch was imported from England."

"Good ticket," murmured Blotto, already excited about the prospect of the next day. It would be the first time in his life that he had played outside the official cricket season. The world could hold no greater attraction for him.

CHAPTER
SEVEN

White Knights v. The Trojan Horse

The vast expanse of Britannia's replica Lord's had a very efficient — and very expensive — watering system so the sacred turf could resist the dehydrating blaze of the Californian sun. That had been working at full power overnight and the grassy surface on to which Blotto stepped the following morning was springy and yet somehow unfamiliar. Now, though his brain was totally inadequate when challenged by anything mildly intellectual — indeed his beaks at Eton had even discussed in the staff room whether he possessed such an organ — in matters of cricket or hunting it matched the speed and perception of his sister's.

He very quickly worked out the difference between what he was standing on and an English pitch. The original surface on which the turf had been laid had not been softened by the incessant rain of his home country. Beneath only a few inches of soil was solid rock.

Blotto nodded sagely. If called upon to bowl he would adjust his action accordingly.

Twinks was fully reconciled to spending the day in front of the Britannia's Pavilion watching cricket. It was a tedium to which someone of her breeding would have to become inured, like sitting through interminable operas, listening to the braying of Old Harrovians or dining with the Royal Family.

She had, needless to say, brought in her trunk a wide variety of wardrobe choices for California. To suit a day's cricket-watching she selected a grey silk dress with a tasselled fringe which revealed a lot of white-stockinged knee when she moved. In a different climate she would have left her arms bare, but under the Californian sun it was wiser to keep them covered. For the same reason, rather than the head-hugging cloche hat she might have worn at the real Lord's, she sported a wide-brimmed straw number with a trailing white silk ribbon around it. Clutched in her hand was the sequined reticule that was always with her. Its contents had helped her and her brother out of many a sticky situation.

Twinks checked her appearance in the Hollywood Hotel mirror before Corky Froggett drove them to Britannia, and even she could not help admitting that she looked stunning. The trip across America in the open Lagonda had brought more colour than usual to her alabaster features.

How tiresome, she thought: that's probably going to lead to even more men falling in love with me.

Twinks was so used to her brother's prowess on the cricket pitch that she hardly noticed how well he played that day for the White Knights (who, incidentally, for people who are interested in that kind of stuff — and the law of averages, if not logic, suggests there must be some — batted first). Unaware of his exceptional abilities, J. Winthrop Stukes had put the newcomer way down the batting order at Number Seven. However, Blotto's call to the wicket came earlier than he might have expected.

And when he went to the crease, he found himself trembling. He wasn't afraid of the opposition's bowling — he wasn't afraid of anyone's bowling — it was who was doing the bowling that made him go weak at the knees.

The opposition's attack was led by a tall, unfeasibly handsome man whom Blotto instantly recognised as Hank Urchief, star of *Chaps' Lonesome Stand* and so many other classic cowboy adventures, and being in the presence of his cinematic hero jangled his nerves. Surely Chaps Chapple, who always emerged triumphant from any kind of glue-pot, would have no problem winning something as minor as a cricket match?

Hank Urchief, it later turned out in conversation, was broadening his range from cowboy roles and actually playing the lead part of Theseus in *The Trojan Horse*. (The fact that Theseus had nothing to do with the Trojan War or the Trojan Horse hadn't troubled the director at all. Gottfried von Klappentrappen wanted to get a Minotaur into his movie, so he rearranged Greek mythology to accommodate that change. It was the Hollywood way. Though they dutifully credited academic advisers on the end credits, everyone in the movie industry knew that mythological and historical accuracy was for sissies. In the same way, von Klappentrappen introduced Jason into the script, because he fancied having a bunch of Argonauts around. Hercules had a bit part too, even though he was Roman rather than Greek. And Helen of Troy only just escaped sharing top billing with Cleopatra.)

Hank Urchief, however, turned out not only to be unfeasibly handsome (which any fan of the Chaps Chapple movies already knew), but also an unfeasibly good bowler. Where he had learnt his cricket from nobody could work out (particularly since he'd been brought up on a turkey farm in Minnesota). Maybe he was just a natural ball-player, maybe it was a skill he was born with. Anyway, its effect was that Saturday at Britannia saw him taking five wickets for eleven runs — he even had Ponky Larreighffriebollaux out for a duck to a sneaky leg-break — which was why Blotto found himself at the batting crease much earlier than he'd expected.

Blotto was still shaking when he faced the first ball from his hero. And as it bulleted past him he made no move to defend his wicket. Fortunately for him, the delivery just missed, though had the left-hand stump had another layer of varnish on it, Devereux Lyminster might have faced a fate unprecedented in his history — registering what was known to the tedious cognoscenti of the game as a "Golden Duck" (out first ball with no score).

Blotto, however, was used to conquering adversity on the cricket pitch. While he might be tongue-tied when he was introduced to Hank Urchief socially, he was fine letting his faithful bat do the talking. He squared up for the next delivery, resolutely erasing from his mind the knowledge that it was being bowled by Chaps Chapple. And he sent the ball over the Pavilion for a six.

After that early lapse, Blotto found his rhythm.

The fact that he stayed there for the rest of the morning and managed to fit a century into the time allotted made J. Winthrop Stukes realise what a rare talent he had on his team.

Twinks was only mildly aware of what was happening out on the pitch. She was much more interested in the other spectators on the seats in front of the Pavilion.

Though her brother had very definitely met Zelda Finch on the S.S. *Regal*, Twinks had not, so she did not recognise the extremely *soignée* lady sitting nearby. Of course, Twinks did not address any remarks to the woman — they had, after all, not been introduced — but when she asked one of the white-coated oriental flunkeys for a glass of iced lemonade, the older woman, hearing her accent, commented, "Oh, you are English?"

Twinks looked through the speaker with an x-ray gaze of which her mother would have been proud.

But Zelda Finch had clearly been away from England too long and caught the infection of American brashness. She continued to speak as though they *had* been introduced, and since she did actually volunteer her name, Twinks considered to reciprocate would not be excessively bad form. Besides, it didn't matter. She was in the United States of America; nobody there would recognise bad form if it came up and bit them on the nose.

"I am Honoria Lyminster," she announced, "though people call me Twinks."

"And may I ask how you come to be here in Hollywood, watching cricket?"

"I'm with him," replied Twinks, gesturing towards Blotto, who had just sent another six over the roof of the Pavilion.

"Oh?" Zelda's tone was icy. The immaculately lipsticked mouth pursed into a small ring of annoyance.

But her mood swiftly changed as Twinks said, "He's my brother."

Zelda's "Ah" was much more friendly. Even though the last time she'd seen him he had placed her on top of the wardrobe in her state room, she still had her eye on Blotto. In fact, he was the reason she'd come to Britannia that morning. She had no more interest in cricket than Twinks had. And though starting an affair with Blotto in Hollywood, under the nose of her notoriously jealous husband, and the glare of publicity spread by gossip columnists like Heddan Schoulders, would not have the anonymity of a dalliance on S.S. *Regal*, the thought of the danger rather excited her.

The thought of Twinks's beauty was rather less appealing. Though she had ruled herself out as a love rival, the girl was still distressingly younger than Zelda Finch, and the actress was very sensitive to the challenge of the young. She immediately saw Twinks as a rival for all those opportunities to be tied to railway lines that no longer came her way.

"Are you actually working on a movie right now?" she asked.

"Working on a movie? Why in the name of strawberries should I be doing that?"

"Well, every beautiful woman who comes to Hollywood wants to be in the movies."

"Not me! The movies are absolutely not my length of banana." Twinks had a patrician contempt for actresses. In her world, their only function was to seduce aristocrats away from their wives. They also had an unfortunate propensity for getting entangled with bishops.

Zelda Finch looked puzzled. "Then why are you here?"

It wasn't the moment to say that she was looking for someone very rich to marry, like, say, a Texas oil millionaire.

Anyway, their conversation was at this point interrupted by the arrival of a tall, rough-hewn man wearing a suit loud enough to necessitate earplugs.

Zelda introduced them. "This is Wilbur T. Cottonpick," she said. "He's a Texas oil millionaire."

As her name was supplied, Twinks held out an exquisitely gloved hand. She was not expecting a kiss on it in the French manner, but then neither was she expecting it to be clenched in quite such a forceful grip. Clearly pulling the black stuff out of the earth — or whatever it was that oilmen did — took a huge amount of strength.

"Hi," said Wilbur T. Cottonpick.

"Mr Cottonpick", said Zelda, "is a man of few words."

"Yup," he confirmed.

"He doesn't believe in using two words where one will do."

"Nope," he confirmed.

At this point the conversation became becalmed, like an incautious pirate ship entering the Saragossa Sea. As another mighty six from her brother flew over their heads, Twinks was beginning to think she might be reduced to actually watching the cricket when Zelda mounted another verbal initiative. "Mr Cottonpick is interested in the commercial possibilities of our national game."

"But it doesn't have any spoffing commercial possibilities," objected Twinks. "That's the whole point of cricket."

"I would point out", said Zelda (who of course, having been brought up in England, knew her stuff when it came to the game), "that cricket has a long history of professional players making a lot of money from their expertise. W. G. Grace would probably be the most famous example."

"Yes, but those were oikish sponge-worms," said Twinks with contempt. "Common people. Not people like us." She looked rather uncertainly at Zelda, not convinced that an actress really could be described as "someone like us", but decided for the moment to give her the benefit of the doubt. "Nobody of breeding would ever contemplate playing cricket simply for the old jingle-jangle."

"I think you'll find — particularly here in America — that there are plenty of people who'd do *anything* for the old jingle-jangle," said Zelda.

Twinks snorted with continuing contempt, then turned to Wilbur T. Cottonpick, who had said nothing during their duologue. "So, you believe there are spondulicks to be garnered from the game of cricket?"

"Yup," he replied.

"And you don't have any worries about meddling with something that's a Grade A foundation stone of the British Empire?"

"Nope," he replied.

"Well, fair biddles to you." In the circumstances, Twinks couldn't think of anything else to say. Though she'd been tempted to riposte with a sharp "Snubbins to you!" But that would have been rude, and she had been brought up to know that rudeness was rarely appropriate with foreigners. They were already suffering so much from the blight of not having been born British that it wasn't really the thing to rub it in.

"Yup," Wilbur T. Cottonpick replied.

"You see," said Zelda, feeling perhaps that further explanation might be required, "there are so many people here in America who have made huge fortunes out of the oil industry and many of them are really stumped when it comes to deciding how to spend all their money."

Well, marrying me would be one way, thought Twinks. But another look at Wilbur T. Cottonpick's suit stopped that idea in its tracks. She was only prepared to go so far in order to bring about the salvation of the Tawcester Towers plumbing.

"A lot", Zelda went on, "invest in the movie business. You've done a bit of that, haven't you, Wilbur?"

"Yup."

"Though sadly none of the movies you've invested in have made any money, have they?"

"Nope."

"But you're pleased about that, aren't you?"

"Yup."

"Because you don't want to make any more money, do you?"

"Nope."

"Just get rid of the stuff?"

"Yup."

"But other Texas oil millionaires", Zelda continued explaining to Twinks, "have bought sports teams . . . baseball . . . American football. You already own the Houston Hoodlums, don't you, Wilbur?"

"Yup."

"And the Dallas Donkeys?"

"Yup."

"And they both lose money, don't they?"

"Yup."

"But not fast enough. You're still making more money than you're losing."

"Yup."

"Which isn't good."

"Nope."

"So," Zelda turned to Twinks. "Wilbur was wondering whether buying a cricket team might be a good way of losing money quicker."

"Well, I'd say it was forty thou to a fishbone he'd be on a winner there," said Twinks.

"She thinks it's a good idea," Zelda translated.

"It's certainly worth having a pop at the partridge," Twinks elaborated.

"Yup," said Wilbur T. Cottonpick.

With each word he spoke, the Texas oil millionaire disqualified himself even further from being, in the view of Twinks, potential husband material. Which was quite an achievement, given how little he said. Zelda had described him as a man of few words. "Three" would have been more accurate.

When the cricket match broke for lunch, J. Winthrop Stukes's team had, thanks to the century from Blotto, an unassailable lead. But, in the view of the two Englishmen, it wasn't thought polite to mention this fact or rub in the inadequacies of their *Trojan Horse* opponents.

The few Americans in the White Knights eleven, however, had no such inhibitions. They gloried in their dominance, jeering as they spelled out the impossibility of the other side beating them. Blotto found it all rather distasteful.

Over pre-prandial drinks, Blotto was properly introduced to Hank Urchief. Being so close to Chaps Chapple, he could produce no words, only mouth like a goldfish. Not that the actor noticed. He was much more interested in Blotto's sister.

At the lunch table Zelda Finch engineered a seat next to Blotto and reintroduced herself. "I'm afraid I was left rather high and dry when we last met," she purred. But there was no reproof in her voice. She behaved as if she regarded being placed on top of a wardrobe on the S.S. *Regal* as a necessary stage in some elaborate courtship ritual.

"Great Wilberforce, yes. Thing the beaks at Eton taught us — when a lady asks you to do something, always tick the box with a big red tick. And never ask the reason why."

"So, if I asked you to do something else for me, Blotto . . . ?" Zelda susurrated.

"I'd be head of the queue with a silver-polished smile."

"I wonder" — her hand hovered over his — "whether you and I could share a little privacy?"

"Tickey-Tockey," said Blotto. "On our own?"

"Exactly that."

"Very well," said Blotto, and he left the room.

Zelda turned in puzzlement to Twinks, who had overheard their exchange. "Now why the hell did he do that?"

"He thought," Blotto's sister explained, "you were asking him to give you a little privacy."

"Oh, rats!" said Zelda Finch, her carmined lips set in a firm line. She was a woman of considerable determination. She hadn't made it through the feuds and betrayals of Hollywood by being passive. She never let herself be depressed by a set-back; it just made her all the more determined to achieve her goal.

And her goal in this case was very definitely Blotto.

The afternoon's proceedings on the cricket pitch were, from Twinks's point of view, mercifully short. J. Winthrop Stukes, impressed as he had been by Blotto's batting, could not imagine that anyone's bowling could be up to the same standard, so it was nearly an hour into the game before he offered Blotto an over. And during that hour, though the rest of the *Trojan Horse* team proved to be uniformly incompetent, Hank Urchief had hogged the batting and was building up a substantial score.

Then Blotto was put on to bowl. He got a hat trick with his first three balls. The next three produced the same result, though Hank Urchief somehow managed to survive. Then another of J. Winthrop Stukes's bowlers was put on. Urchief hit three sixes off him, and scored a single at the end of the over so that he would once again be facing the bowling. The last man at the other end was a rather nervous Argonaut.

Blotto started his run-up at the beginning of his second over. Adjusting again to the surface of grass-covered rock, he sent down a delivery that had the ferocity of a cannon ball.

Hank Urchief's middle stump splintered into fragments as it spun out of the ground.

The game was over. Had the vulgar concept of "Man of the Match" been invented in those days, Blotto would undoubtedly have won it.

Zelda Finch made her way through the ecstatic crowd of his fellow players and sibilated into his ear, "There's going to be a wild party at Mimsy La Pim's tonight. You must come."

The invitation could not have been more welcome to Blotto's ears. The perfect day's cricket was to be crowned by a meeting with the woman of his black and white dreams.

CHAPTER
EIGHT

Party People

Mimsy La Pim lived in a mansion. It seemed that everyone in Hollywood lived in a mansion, or at least a Hollywood set designer's idea of what a mansion might look like. Hers had a kind of Spanish flavour — think Cordoba meets *Zorro*. It was as if a humble pueblo-style building of white walls and clay-tile roofs had been given an overdose of growth hormone. Every courtyard or patio led to another courtyard or patio. No room lacked for alcoves and niches; no alcove or niche was unadorned by terracotta ornaments. Any wall that could be covered with ceramic tiles was covered with ceramic tiles. Thick studded wooden doors stood in every doorway. You couldn't move for ornamental ironwork. Guitars, sombreros and straw donkeys were propped in every corner.

But it was clearly a great place for a party. Though the Californian sun had set, the Californian heat saw no reason to go to bed early. The front of the house was illuminated by a thousand candles. And as the Lagonda approached up the drive, its passengers heard the shrieking and posing of Mimsy La Pim's guests rise in volume. Somewhere in the bowels of the mansion cool jazz was playing.

Everyone who was anyone in Hollywood was there, along with a few people who weren't really anyone anywhere but who always turned up to parties. People who were famous stood around looking famous, and people who weren't quite famous postured around trying to look famous. Among the guests, the permutations of lovers, prospective lovers and ex-lovers were so complicated they couldn't have been calculated on the most advanced slide rules or logarithmic tables of the day.

And into this maelstrom of celebrity Blotto and Twinks were delivered by Corky Froggett at the entrance to Mimsy La Pim's mansion.

Of their hostess Blotto was disappointed to find no sign, but he was soon swept up by Zelda Finch who had been on the lookout for him. Though the party boasted the most famous faces and bodies in the world, there was no question that Twinks looked more beautiful than any of them. She was approached simultaneously by Toni Frangipani, Hank Urchief and Wilbur T. Cottonpick, who vied with each other, snapping fingers at waiters to get her a drink. The disregard for Prohibition was as evident here as it had been elsewhere in Hollywood. And perhaps part of the explanation lay in the numbers of senior police officers who were present, downing Mimsy La Pim's alcohol.

Zelda's hand was tightly shackling Blotto's arm as she whisked him through the crowd. "Soon we will be alone," she murmured, "and then we can make sweet music."

"Ah, bit of a chock in the cogwheel there," said Blotto. "You see, the beaks at Eton found this out when they tried to get me to sing along to 'Jolly Boating Weather'. Fact is, not to twiddle round the turnips, I'm tone deaf."

Zelda might have pursued her innuendo further but for the fact that they suddenly found themselves confronted by a small man with a monocle, jodhpurs and a riding crop. Blotto, who was far too well brought up to mention such details, could not help observing that he had a body with the contours of a tennis ball and a face like a boiled prawn.

"Ah," said Zelda. "You haven't met. This is my husband."

The short man thrust out a pugnacious, stubby hand and said teutonically, "I'm Gottfried von Klappentrappen."

"Sorry to put an earthworm in the salad," said Blotto, "but I'm afraid that's wrong."

The director, who was very unused to being told he was wrong about anything, could only echo the word. "Wrong?"

"Bong on the nose, yes. Out here in America you don't say 'Gottfried'," Blotto explained helpfully. "You say 'Gottenfried'."

The director exploded with a cry of "*Gott im Himmel!*"

"That's right." Blotto smiled reassuringly. "You've gotten it."

*   *   *

"You must letta me show you arounda Hollywood," Toni Frangipani said to Twinks.

"You must let *me* show you around Hollywood," said Hank Urchief.

"Yup," said Wilbur T. Cottonpick.

"Larksissimo!" Twinks turned the full power of her azure eyes on Hank Urchief. "It'd be absolutely the lark's larynx to be shown round Hollywood by *you*."

"Great," said Hank Urchief. "Tomorrow morning I'll take you on the set of *The Trojan Horse* at Humungous Studios."

"Jollissimo!" said Twinks. "I will look forward to it like an egg does to Easter."

But Toni Frangipani was not pleased with the direction of the conversation — nor of Twinks's azure eyes. "Hey, you don't wanna see that *Trojan Horsa* garbage. Tomorrowa morning I takea you on to the setta of my latest movie at Elephantine Studios, *The Sheik of the Sahara*. Thatsa going to be really bigga at the boxa office. Mr Cottonpick here, he's a bigga investor in it."

"Yup," said Wilbur T. Cottonpick.

"I think", said Twinks, channelling her mother's *froideur*, "that I would prefer to talk in private with Mr Urchief than with you two gentlemen." There was silence. "Do you have a mousesqueak of an idea what I'm saying?"

"Yup," said Wilbur T. Cottonpick.

The Italian actor looked at him in amazement. "Is thissa woman givinga me, Toni Frangipani, the bumsa rush?"

"Yup," said Wilbur T. Cottonpick.

Toni's dark complexion turned almost black with fury. As he and Wilbur T. Cottonpick, having taken Twinks's not very subtle hint, moved away from her, Toni Frangipani looked across to a table where the two bulky Mediterranean types who had watched over him on S.S. *Regal* were sitting. One of the men pointed towards Twinks, made a throat-cutting gesture and looked interrogatively at his boss. Toni Frangipani shook his head and executed a very expressive hand gesture — he was good at gesturing from his silent work in front of the camera — which very clearly gave the message: "Soona, but notta quitea yetta."

Twinks was pleased to be alone with Hank Urchief. She had taken quite a shine to him at the cricket match and relished the opportunity to talk to him further. Also, as one of Hollywood's hottest stars, he was undoubtedly rich enough to qualify as potential husband material.

He plucked two glasses of champagne for them from a passing tray and led her into a sheltered courtyard redolent of orange trees. Here the jazz was inaudible, but in a shady corner a man with a sombrero plucked out yearning tunes on a guitar. Hank gestured for Twinks to sit on a rustic bench and joined her, close enough for her to feel the ripple of his muscular thigh against hers.

"So . . ." he said, "we didn't really get a chance to talk at the match."

"No," she agreed. "You played like a Leamington lizard." Hank shrugged at the compliment. "Have you played a lot of cricket?"

"Coupla times with J. Winthrop Stukes's set-up."

"Not before? Not when you were at school?"

"Ain't no school here in the States that teaches cricket. I didn't go to school too often, anyway. Not much of a one for book-larning. I was brought up on a turkey farm in Minnesota."

"Well, when it comes to cricket, you're as natural as a baby's smile."

He responded with a self-depreciating "Shucks." Then he turned the full focus of his dark eyes (black, of course, on the screen, but deep brown in reality). "So tell me, Twinks, what movie are you working on?"

It was the same question Zelda Finch had asked her. Mildly irritated, she replied that she wasn't working on any movie.

"Then why else is someone as purty as you out here in Hollywood?"

Once again, it didn't do to say, I'm looking for a rich husband. Like you perhaps. So Twinks fudged, "Oh, I'm really here just as a companionette to my brother while he plays cricket."

"He's sure got some talent. Is he an all-rounder?"

"Well, you saw that, didn't you? Blotto's a Grade A whale in both the batting and the bowling departments."

"No, I meant, is he an all-rounder in the sense of being good at everything? Has he got the brains to match his sporting talent?"

Twinks thought it was time to move the conversation on. "This house is absolutely the lark's larynx, isn't it?"

"Oh, sure." Hank shrugged. "Bit small by Hollywood standards."

"Have you got a bigger spread?"

"Too right I have. Could fit two of this little shack into mine."

"I did once meet Mimsy La Pim on the French Riviera. She must be pulling in the jingle-jangle to own a place like this."

"Wouldn't be too sure about that."

"Oh?"

"Hollywood can be a cruel place. One day you're the toast of every producer in town, next day you're just toast."

"Really? You mean Mimsy La Pim's career is skidding down the slippery slope to oblivion?"

Hank Urchief nodded. "That's about the size of it. Her agent's phone's gone silent. There've just opened up a new can of younger, prettier actresses to tie to railway lines."

"Are you saying that Mimsy might have to move out of this place?"

"No, she's all right, so long as she's got Lennie to protect her."

"Lennie?"

"Lenny 'The Skull' Orvieto, the Mafia boss. Mimsy La Pim's his current bit of skirt."

Twinks was silent, thinking how desolated her brother would be to hear that news.

But before anything else was said, the couple were interrupted by a cry of "Hold the front page! And the back page! And all the pageroonies in between! Hunky heartthrob Hank Urchief seen in cheeky clinch with new baberoonie starlet!"

The woman who approached them was tall, wearing a scarlet dress with high lapels and a matching hat the size of a traction engine wheel.

"I am not," said Twinks, once again showing a disturbing family likeness to her mother, "'a new baberoonie starlet'. Nor am I in a 'cheeky clinch' with anyone."

Hank Urchief grinned. "Don't worry, babe —"

"I am no more a 'babe' than I am a 'baberoonie'!"

"Don't let it get to you," he said. "It's just how she talks all the time. Let me introduce you. I've forgotten your proper name."

"Honoria Lyminster," came the icy reply. "I am the daughter of the late Duke and the sister of the current Duke of Tawcester."

Hank Urchief gestured to the two women. "Honoria Lyminster, this is Heddan Schoulders, who is just about the most famous gossip columnist Hollywood has ever seen."

"Hey, Hank, what's with the 'just about'?" the woman screeched. "Heddan Schoulders *is* the most famous gossip columnist Hollywood has ever seen. Hell, Heddan Schoulders *invented* the job!"

"If you say so."

"I *do* say so! And don't you forget, Hank Urchief, that I was the one who put you on the Hollywood map. Didn't I? With that first interview I did with you, when you were just a poor boy from a turkey farm in Minnesota."

"I've always been grateful to you for that," he admitted.

"Do you remember the headline I wrote for that interview?"

"I sure do."

"'SLICK HICK CLIX IN PIX!'" Heddan Schoulders recalled proudly.

"I'll never forget it."

"Anyway," she said, turning to Twinks, "always a big buzz to see a new face in Hollywood. The old ones are looking so tired — even the ones that have been lifted. In fact, especially the ones that have been lifted. But yours is a stunner. 'STUNNER STARLET SECRETLY SNAFFLES SEXY HUNK HANK.' That'll be the headline for my column."

"Oh, for the love of strawberries, I'm not snaffling anyone!"

"So, Honoria, spill me all those beans about what slick flick you're strutting your stuff in?"

"Is there nobody out here in Hollywood who can read my semaphore?" Twinks demanded despairingly. "I am not in any movie! I am not an actress! I can't act!"

"Couldn't matter less," Heddan Schoulders reassured her. "Being able to act just gets in the way. All you have to do is stand in front of the camera and make the faces the director tells you to. A cauliflower could do it."

"Better than a lotta the people who are doing it," commented Hank Urchief. "And a cauliflower would

82

get as much fan mail. You'd have to write about the dirty doings of cauliflowers in your column, Hedda."

"I'll believe that when it happens. Mind you," she went on, "when the talkies come in, that'll weed out the cauliflowers who can't act. And the ones who can't speak English. And the ones with squeaky voices."

"It'll never happen," said Hank. "It's just a gimmick."

"Oh yeah? They're testing out a new sound system at Warner Brothers. It'll come."

"And men'll walk on the moon," said Hank dismissively.

"Just you wait. The movies will always be a glamorarium and . . ." said Hedda, turning back to Twinks, "you got glamour in barrowloads. Someone picture-book pretty like you *must* be in the movies. Hank, surely there's a part for this dreamcake in *The Trojan Horse*?"

"There might just be. I heard about an hour ago that Lita Bottel, our Helen of Troy, has been arrested for shooting her Mexican pool boy."

"Hey, that's great. Why didn't you tell me sooner?"

"I've hardly had a chance to —"

" 'LOVE TRIANGLE SHOOTING STAR TOTALS UNDERAGE LOVER'!" Heddan Schoulders announced. "That'll be my headline for the pool boy story."

"But do you know that Lita Bottel was involved in a love triangle?" asked Twinks.

"Oh, purr-leeze . . ." said Heddan Schoulders. "I'm a gossip columnist. I don't do truth."

Hank Urchief elaborated. "Here in Hollywood, Twinks, publicity is what matters. Nobody gives a damn whether what's reported is accurate. Just so long as it keeps your name fresh in the public consciousness."

"Well, I think that's fumacious," said Twinks, uncharacteristically prissy. "In England we believe in telling the truth at all times."

"Yeah? Even in the newspapers?"

"Well, not in the newspapers, obviously."

"And was the success of the British Empire," asked Hank sardonically, "always based on telling the truth to the natives whose lands they seized? Like, say, the native tribes who lived here before the Pilgrim Fathers arrived?"

Twinks was beginning to feel she'd got off on the wrong foot and that the conversation might be improved by a change of subject. "Anyway, I'll be pretty vinegared off if I find any lies about me appearing in a gossip column."

"It's not something over which you have any control," said Hank, and Heddan chuckled in agreement.

"You mean gossip columnists can write whatever they want about people?"

"Sure can." Heddan Schoulders nodded complacently.

"Don't you have libel lawyers out here?"

"Oh, hell yes, Twinks," said Hank. "Hollywood is full of lawyers of every kind. You can't move for them. There are probably at least fifty at this party. And a lotta them are very good at taking libel cases to court."

"To ensure that justice is seen to be done?" suggested Twinks.

"Hell, no. To get more publicity. All going to court ensures is that the libel gets repeated by everyone in Hollywood."

"Well, Heddan," Twinks turned to the gossip columnist, "it so happens that I don't wish you to write anything about me. I'm appealing to your better nature."

"Don't have one," came the reply. "And listen, babe, you're a story. Nothing in the world's going to stop me writing about you."

"No?"

"No." Inspiration glowed in Heddan Schoulders' eyes. "And I've got the perfect headline for you."

"What?" asked Twinks wearily.

"HUNK HANK CASTS BRIT ARISTO SQUEEZE AS HELEN IN *TROJAN HORSE* FLICK."

"Oh, stuff a pillow in it!" said Twinks.

CHAPTER
NINE

Virtue in Danger?

Blotto still hadn't seen any sign of Mimsy La Pim. Nor, after being introduced to and removed from the company of her husband, had he managed to evade the close surveillance of Zelda Finch, who kept plying him with alcohol, mostly very fine single malt whiskies, desecrated with ice, from the trays of the passing waiters.

He didn't dislike Zelda, he just wasn't very interested in her. And he found it enormously frustrating actually to be in Mimsy La Pim's home without yet having had a sight of his hostess. But the *politesse* of his upbringing prevented him from telling Zelda of his feelings. He had been taught enough about women to know that, generally speaking, they didn't like men talking exclusively about other women in their presence. If Zelda raised the subject of Mimsy, then fine, but if not, his frustration would just have to continue. Sometimes, he thought not for the first time, it was hell being a British gentleman.

He was encouraged, however, when Zelda suggested they go upstairs. Maybe she was catching on to what he really wanted to do. The owner of a house was much more likely to be upstairs than any of her guests. Perhaps Zelda was leading him towards Mimsy.

She certainly seemed to be looking for someone. On the landing with its long wrought-iron railings she kept opening bedroom doors and then closing them very quickly when she heard squeals and shrieks from inside.

Finally, she found one that seemed to be unoccupied and led Blotto inside. The room was huge, and the bed, with wrought-iron details at its head and foot, was also enormous. Even huger were the stout wooden doors that enclosed the wardrobe.

"You are about to find what you've always been looking for," Zelda sultried.

"Toad in the hole!" said Blotto, for whom things seemed suddenly to be getting better.

"Sit on the bed, darling," said Zelda, "while I organise something that will make your evening even better."

Obediently he sat on the bed, but he was slightly puzzled by what she did next. He couldn't see what it had to do with finding Mimsy when she got a small package out of her handbag and lay lines of its white powdered contents on the glass surface of the dressing table. Nor did her producing a fifty-dollar note and rolling it into a tube seem likely to bring his idol any closer. Still, he also knew it wasn't polite to question the actions of a lady. They had their own rules of behaviour, inexplicable to the understanding of the average male.

"Have you done this before?" asked Zelda.

Blotto wasn't sure what she was referring to, but a "Great Wilberforce, no!" seemed to cover most possible eventualities.

"It's very easy, and it'll really give you a buzz," said Zelda. "You know what this is, don't you?"

"White powder," Blotto hazarded.

"Sure it's white powder, and white powder that'll really blow the top off your head."

"Good ticket," he said, slightly uncertain.

"Powder for the nose."

Finally understanding, he nodded and said, "On the same page."

"Powder to put up your nose."

Blotto chuckled. "Ah, now you're jiggling my kneecap."

"What?"

"You're taking me for a starling with half an eggshell still on its head."

"Sorry?"

"Look, Zelda, I may not know a lot about the whole rombooley of things ladies get up to in the privacy of their *toilettes*, but I've been in my sister's boudoir often enough to be sure of one thing."

"And what's that?"

"Ladies don't put powder *up* their noses, they put it *on* their noses, usually with a powder-puff."

Zelda Finch's eyes rolled heavenwards as she bent down towards the line of white powder and snorted the whole lot up the fifty-dollar bill into her nose. She was still for a moment, waiting to feel the effect, then proffered the improvised tube to Blotto. "D'you want to . . .?"

He chortled at the incongruity of her suggestion. "Boddoes in England, you've clearly forgotten, don't use make-up. It may be the thing over here in Hollywood, but if any of my old muffin-toasters from Eton heard I'd been using face powder . . . well, they'd definitely think my banana was bending the wrong way."

Zelda gave up. She threw the bank note down on to the dressing table and draped herself languorously over the huge bed. "Well now, Blotto," she throbbed, "I think it's time I really gave you what you want."

"That'd be really fizzulating, my old fruitcake," he admitted.

She patted the coverlet beside her. "Come and sit here."

"Tickey-Tockey," he said. He couldn't think why she wanted him to sit there, but once again it didn't do to question a lady's instructions.

Zelda Finch laid an expensively manicured hand on his muscular thigh. "You see, I know what you want, Blotto . . ."

"Good ticket."

". . . possibly better than you know yourself."

"Well, I do know myself quite well," he objected. "I mean, I have been sort of hanging round myself for a very long —"

"Don't let's get caught up in words, Blotto. Let's cut to the chase."

"Hoopee-doopee!" he said.

"You came to Hollywood looking for something, didn't you, Blotto?"

"Well, the stated purpose of the visit was to play cricket."

"I know that, but there was something else you were really hoping to find."

Blotto looked a little shamefaced. "Gosh, you see through a boddo like a medic with a microscope."

"I think it's fair to say I have a pretty good understanding of human psychology — particularly masculine psychology."

"Double echo to that, Zelda."

"You really came to Hollywood looking for a woman . . ."

"Well, I'll be snickered."

"The woman of your dreams . . ."

"You're bong on the nose there," he admitted.

"A woman whose image you have admired ever since you first saw it flicker across the silver screen."

"This is spookiferous, Zelda. It's like you've got a front stalls ticket to my brain."

"As I said, I always know what men are thinking. It's not too difficult, actually. In ninety-nine cases out of a hundred, the old adage about men only thinking about one thing turns out to be true."

Feeling some kind of appropriate comment was required, Blotto fell back on, "Beezer."

The hand on his thigh was now stroking vigorously. "And isn't it marvellous, Blotto," Zelda purred, "that you've found what you are looking for right here."

"Here?"

90

"Here, in this very room."

"Toad in the hole!" he exclaimed. "Here in this very room?"

He sprang up from the bed, crossed the room in two strides and pulled the massive wardrobe doors open . . . to reveal nothing but a selection of expensive clothes.

He turned back in disappointment to face Zelda Finch.

"So where is Mimsy?" he asked.

Mimsy La Pim's absence from her own party had now become an obsession with Blotto. It was something that demanded an explanation. Everything within told him that he had to find her.

He did not notice the expression of pique on Zelda Finch's face as he swept out of the bedroom. Opening every other door on the landing, he took no notice of the embarrassing combinations of movie stars he found within (there were enough to keep Heddan Schoulders in scurrilous columns for a year). All that registered with Blotto was the fact that none of the bedrooms contained Mimsy La Pim.

He went downstairs again and trawled through the posturing crowds in the interlocking corridors and courtyards, but still with no result. In the humid candlelit gardens and on the tiled edges of the two swimming pools he still found nothing that resembled Mimsy.

He asked everyone he encountered, but no one seemed to have seen her.

Eventually he decided it was worth checking out the servants' quarters.

And there, in one of the huge kitchens, he found it.

A sheet of paper pinned to a huge oak table by a vicious-looking knife.

On it were scrawled the words: "WE'VE GOT MIMSY LA PIM. YOU WILL BE CONTACTED ABOUT THE RANSOM ARRANGEMENTS."

Blotto shuddered. Mimsy La Pim had been kidnapped!

CHAPTER
TEN

A Chivalrous Quest

Blotto looked impossibly noble as he announced, "Now I have a quest. Like one of the knights of King Arthur's Round Table. Like Sir Gallipot."

"Galahad," his sister suggested gently.

"Yes, one of those greengages, anyway."

They were in Twinks's suite at the Hollywood Hotel the day after the disappearance of Mimsy La Pim. For a moment Blotto's expression was tinged with regret. "Wish I had Mephistopheles here with me."

Twinks knew he was referring to his hunter, safely stabled back at Tawcester Towers. "Why, in the name of strawberries, do you want him out here? Do they hunt in California as well as play cricket?"

Blotto was sidetracked for a moment by the attraction of the idea. "Crusty crumpets, I wonder if they do . . .? It'd be a beezer wheeze if they did. Then a boddo could hunt here when it was closed season back in old GB . . . as well as playing cricket all year round. You know, I may have said some tinglish things about the US of A at times, but in some ways it's a spoffing well-organised society."

Twinks brought him back to the subject in hand. "You were talking about Sir Galahad, not Mephistopheles . . ."

"Yes, Twinks me old bootscraper, but the two are connected."

"Oh?"

"I'd feel more like the gallant Sir Galahad setting out on a quest if I was on a horse."

"Riding a horse on the streets of Los Angeles, you'd stick out like a puppy in a basket of kittens."

"You're right, sis," he said regretfully. "I'll have to put the candle-snuffer on that idea."

"And you weren't thinking of decking yourself out in full armour, too, were you?"

"Great Wilberforce, no!" Blotto lied.

He noticed the pile of newspapers scattered over his sister's dressing table. "Anything in any of those smut-rags about Mimsy's disappearance?"

"That's what I was running the peepers over them for. But since it only happened yesterday, few of them have caught up." She picked up a newspaper. "Only snoop who's on the case is — no surprise there — Heddan Schoulders."

"Who's she?"

"Oh, you didn't meet her at last night's bunfest, did you? Heddan Schoulders is, according to herself, *the* biggest gossip columnist in Hollywood. And, of course, because she was actually *at* Mimsy La Pim's last night, she's got the exclusive."

Twinks read out:

MOLL MIMSY HOME PATCH SNATCH
IN SMARTY PARTY GLITZ BLITZ

Mimsy La Pim, one-time doe-eyed doll, now more of a made-man's moll, gave a party last night at her own hacienda. But hacienda the good news for Mimsy! She shoulda been the hostess with the mostest, but she ended the evening the hostess who was lostest. Kidded and caught napping by kidnappers at her own home! Duct-taped around the mouth and abducted! The LAPD are on the case, but we all know they're so slow they'd be LAPPED in a tortoise race. Mimsy La Pim's been saved from a fate worse than death many times on the silver screen, but who's going to save her from the real thing?

"I am," said Blotto devoutly. "It's my quest."
Twinks raised her beautiful eyelashes to glance at her brother before continuing her reading.

But why did the kidnapping happen? Has 'butter-wouldn't-melt-in-her-mouth' Mimsy been butting into places where she didn't ought to have butt? Has she committed the offence of offending a rather important Caporoonie called Lenny? Or are some other Cosaroonies who don't see eye to eye with Lenny giving him one in the eye by snatching Mimsy? As soon as the news cues, you know you'll hear it here first from your alter-ego amigo Heddan Schoulders!

"Toad in the hole!" said Blotto. "A lot of spoffing wocky wordage comes out of her tooth-box, doesn't it, Twinks me old bathplug? You'd think a journalist would have learned to speak proper English like we do, wouldn't you?"

"You're on the right side of right there, Blotto me old griddle-pan," his sister agreed.

"Who's this LAPD she was pongling on about?"

"Los Angeles Police Department."

"Ah. Should we ask them how they're getting on with the investigation?"

Twinks shook her head decisively. "Police out here don't take kindly to amateur investigators."

"Toad in the hole!" said Blotto. "Back in the old GB they couldn't be more helpful." He thought fondly of Chief Inspector Trumbull and Sergeant Knatchbull of the Tawcestershire Constabulary back in England. "The only function of the police in Blighty is to be permanently baffled."

"Bit different out here," said Twinks. "If we investigate Mimsy La Pim's kidnap we're going to have to be as secret as a mistress at a family party."

"Oh? Why?"

"Because, apart from the local cops not liking amateurs, Blotto me old tub of shaving soap, there could be some real stenchers in the Force who are actually responsible for Mimsy's disappearance."

"Toad in the hole! Do you know something about it?" He was used to his sister having inside information on almost everything. "Come on, uncage the ferrets."

Twinks had to be careful. After what she had heard from Hank Urchief, she felt convinced there was a Mafia connection to Mimsy La Pim's kidnapping, but she didn't want to reveal to her brother that the actress was Lenny "The Skull" Orvieto's "current bit of skirt." So all she said was, "There's a criminal underworld in Hollywood."

"Is there?" said Blotto. "Kind of like a subway? So how do you get down into it?"

"No, no. It's not a real underworld. It's a metaphor."

"Ah yes," Blotto responded airily, "I remember discussing those with Ponky Larreighffriebollaux."

"Did you really?" The idea of the two of them discussing figures of speech sounded unlikely, but Twinks pressed on. "The fact is, Blotto, that wherever there are spondulicks to be made, then you're going to get some fumacious criminals muscling in on the shooting party. And because there are Jereboamsful of spondulicks to be made in Hollywood, it means there are Jereboamsful of fumacious criminals trying to get their hands on it."

"Do you know which fumacious criminals might be after Mimsy?" asked Blotto.

"I think they may be of Italian origin."

Blotto nodded sagely. "That would fit the pigeonhole, yes."

"Sorry, not on the same page, Blotters?"

"Well, a lot of Italian boddoes have moustaches, don't they?"

"Ye-es," Twinks agreed cautiously.

"So the stenchers could twirl them . . ."

"Ye-es."

". . . while they tied her to railway lines."

For a moment Twinks was tempted to spell out to her brother the difference between the movies and real life, but then she decided it really wasn't worth the effort. "What I was really talking about, Blotto me old soap rack, was . . ." She lowered her voice. "Can I say the word 'Mafia'?"

"Yes, you can," said Blotto.

"What do you mean?"

"Well, you just did."

"Did what?"

"Say the word 'Mafia'. Came across loud and clear into my lug-sockets. Don't don your worry-boots about that, old thing. You can certainly say the word. 'Mafia', no doubt about it. You could probably represent England in a Mafia-saying competition."

"But what I meant was —"

Her brother, however, had already moved on. "Anyway, I can't think about stuff like that now," he said. "I have a higher calling. It is now my sacred quest to rescue Mimsy, just like Sir Gastropod."

"Galahad," said Twinks wearily.

She was about to throw the paper down when another item at the bottom of Hedda's column caught her eye. "Oh, for the love of apricots . . ." she said.

Twinks didn't usually employ such strong language, but then rarely had she been so provoked. The headline read,

"HUNK HANK CASTS BRIT ARISTO SQUEEZE AS HELEN IN *TROJAN HORSE* FLICK".

In a state of some trepidation she read on:

Languorous Lita Bottel did something oopsadaisical by shooting her jail-bait pool boy cuddle in love triangle. But moviemeister Gottfried von Klappentrappen isn't prepared to wait till she gets out of the slammer to do his own bitta shooting on his Humungous Studios *Trojan Horse* extravaganzaroonie. So it's bye-bye, old Helen of Troy, and how ya doing, new Helen of Troy? Then who is to be the face who launched a thousand gossip columns? Wouldja believe that once again it's your press princess Heddan Schoulders who got the exclusive! Maybe it's because brawny beefcake Hank Urchief was brought up on a turkey farm in Minnesota that he's lost his taste for the birds Hollywood Boulevard has on offer and is now touching toes with an English rose. Yup, to be frank, Hank the Yank's on the swank, getting red-blooded with a blue-blooded Brit chit. She's a close confidante of the English King, called Lady Honoria Lemondrop, Duchess of Tastebud, whose family history goes as far back as the Civil War (theirs, not ours, dumbos). And she's the new Helen of Troy over whom flickslicker Gottfried von Klappentrappen will be cracking his riding crop on the *Trojan Horse* set tomorrow. Admit it, you'd be no-news numbskulls if you didn't have your colossal columnist Heddan Schoulders telling it straightest and keeping up with the latest, wouldntja? Till the next time, you-all!

"Oh, rodents!" said Twinks, again using stronger language than was her well-bred wont. "Why do the press always get everything wrong?"

"May I clap my peepers on it?" asked Blotto.

With a despairing sigh, Twinks chucked the paper over to her brother.

There was a long silence — Blotto never had been a quick reader. Eventually, he said, "You're right, Twinks me old soup ladle. They have got it wrong. Our family doesn't go back to the Civil War. It goes back to the Norman Conquest."

"If that was the only thing they'd clunked up . . ." said Twinks hopelessly.

"But you are going to do it, aren't you?" asked Blotto.

"What?"

"Step up to the crease as Helen of Troy?"

"Blotto me old mashie niblick, I'm as likely to play Helen of Troy as the Mater is to join a travelling circus."

"Oh."

Twinks immediately identified the disappointment in his monosyllable. "Blotters, what's put lumps in your custard?"

"Well, I was just thinking . . . how're we going to crank up the engine on our quest to find Mimsy La Pim." Twinks was too tender-spirited to point out that it was actually *his* not *our* quest. "We're not overstocked with leads . . . and most of the people we know in Hollywood . . . Gottenfried von Klappentrappen, Zelda Finch, Hank Urchief, J. Winthrop Stukes . . . well, they're all in some way bingled up with this *Trojan Horse* rombooley."

100

"So you're suggesting, Blotto, that I should take the part of Helen of Troy simply so I can help investigate the disappearance of Mimsy La Pim?"

"You're bong on the nose there, Twinks." He was relieved that his sister had so readily got the point, but her expression wasn't encouraging.

"There is one tiny problemette, though, Blotters . . ." she replied.

"And what's that when it's got its spats on?"

"In spite of what Heddan Schoulders' column murbled on about, I haven't yet been *offered* the part of Helen of Troy."

At that moment the phone in the suite rang. It was Gottfried von Klappentrappen, offering Honoria Lyminster the part of Helen of Troy. Twinks accepted.

There was a sparkle in her eye as she put down the receiver and looked back at her brother. "You were right, Blotto. This *is* going to be the best way to advance our investigation. And I think the whole clangdumble is going to be larksissimo!"

"Good ticket," said Blotto.

CHAPTER
ELEVEN

On the Set of
The Trojan Horse

"*Gott im Himmel!*" shrieked Gottfried von Klappentrappen once again. "Just stand still! If you move
your head, vee don't see zee snakes move!"

The studio in which he was working was huge and
filled with a set designer's idea of what Ancient Greece
— or possibly Ancient Rome — might have looked like.
The basic principle on which he or she seemed to have
worked was that you can never have too many stone
columns. Many more columns would be built when
Gottfried von Klappentrappen moved out of the studio
and started location filming, marshalling the thousands
of extras who were a feature of every movie he made.

That morning in the studio he was beginning to lose
his temper while setting up a complicated shot
featuring Medusa. With the level of punctilious
attention that Hollywood brought to everything except
historical accuracy, it had been decided that Medusa's
hair of snakes should be made of real snakes. Sadly, the
actress playing the part was ophidiophobic (though, for
obvious reasons, Twinks wouldn't say that to Blotto

when she recounted the scene to him later in the day — he wouldn't have a clue what she was talking about — she'd just say the actress was terrified of snakes). The result was that every time her living wig was put on her head she trembled so much it was impossible to get a decent shot of her. Which was why Gottfried von Klappentrappen was bawling her out.

What made the situation exciting for the film crew (including the one who was paid by Heddan Schoulders to inform her of any on-set dirt) was that the actress playing Medusa was Zelda Finch, which meant the director was bawling out his wife. Already one of the lighting technicians was running a book on how long von Klappentrappen's latest marriage would last. Separation before the end of the month was odds-on.

This speculation was fuelled by further gossip from a minor starlet called Buza Cruz. (She was playing a lady at the court of King Theseus, whose only scene involved being turned to stone by Medusa's stare — something that required very little effort since Buza's acting talent stretched no further than permanently looking as if she'd been turned to stone.)

Buza, however, had been at Mimsy La Pim's party a couple of nights before. And she swore she'd seen Zelda Finch go into one of the upstairs bedrooms, followed a little while later by a tall young man with blond hair. Given the way news spreads on a film set, it was only a matter of time before von Klappentrappen heard the rumours. He heard them all right but, frustratingly, he didn't know the precise details. And he felt that asking Buza Cruz directly to expand her insinuations would dilute the man-of-the-world coolness he thought essential to his image as a Hollywood film director.

Another of the lighting technicians was already running a book on what form, once von Klappentrappen had identified the young man in question, the notoriously jealous director's revenge would take.

Meanwhile, looking increasingly like a demented onion in his khaki shirt, jodhpurs and monocle, Gottfried von Klappentrappen strutted and stormed around.

On the *Trojan Horse* set at Humungous Studios, Twinks watched these goings-on from a distance. So far she had no complaints about the way she'd been treated. A limousine had picked her up at the Hollywood Hotel and delivered her to the studios. At the security barrier a gateman had waved her vehicle through after consulting a collection of photographs in his booth. Hollywood stars had a strong aversion to not being recognised, and studio security staff had always to be on their guard against asking for ID from somebody famous. Had Twinks realised — or had she cared about such things — the fact that her photograph was in the gateman's collection was a very good sign for the future of her movie career. She was already being treated as a star.

And it has to be said that on set she looked the part. In her Helen of Troy costume and make-up, she appeared even more like a Greek goddess than usual.

She was sitting with J. Winthrop Stukes, who was almost invisible behind the heavy wigging and bearding of Methuselah. (It was a Hollywood convention that age was represented by wigs and beards, the older the character the longer the wig and beard. Methuselah had been given hair to match his longevity, so much of the stuff that Stukes was in constant danger of tripping over it.)

For someone like Twinks, who had only ever seen a silent film accompanied by music in a picture house, the set was surprisingly noisy. And the dominant noise was Gottfried von Klappentrappen's shouting.

Hank Urchief, who had been coming on to Twinks all morning, had recently left their little group, and she watched him as he crossed towards two haggard-looking men seated in folding canvas chairs way behind von Klappentrappen and his cameras. Tweed suits hung from both their perished frames, both were losing their hair and what was left was untidy, as if a lot of it had just been torn out. In the hollow eyes of both men glinted the light of paranoia.

"Who are those two bliss-bereft boddoes?" asked Twinks.

J. Winthrop Stukes looked across. "Ah," he said, "the one on the right, who Hank's talking to, is Paul Uckliss-Hack."

"And what does the wretched thimble do? He looks as if topping himself would be high on his list of priorities."

"You're not far off the mark, young lady. He's the writer."

"Oh, the poor droplet." Twinks had been in Hollywood long enough to know the legacy of misery that came with that role.

"And it looks," Stukes observed, "as though Hank is telling him to do another rewrite."

"But surely Hank has no right to do that?"

The old actor grinned wryly. "You've got a lot to learn, young lady. *Everyone* has the right to tell the writer to do another rewrite. The director, obviously. The stars, obviously. Perhaps less obviously, the supporting actors. The walk-ons. The technicians. The wardrobe personnel. The make-up people. The set designers. The lighting technicians. The studio cat. In fact, I think you'll find that one of the snakes in Medusa's wig has the right to ask the writer for a rewrite."

"Ah. No wonder Paul Uckliss-Hack looks like he's swallowed the whole lemon. What about the other poor pineapple? Looks as if he's got even more lumps in his custard."

"Ah. He is an extremely eminent academic. His name's Professor Gervase Blunkett-Plunkett. He's the Egregious Professor of History at Oxford University."

"And which pigeonhole does he fit into on *The Trojan Horse*?"

"He's the classical adviser. He's here to see that no liberties are taken with the facts of history or mythology."

Twinks nodded. She didn't need any further explanation of the despair that overwhelmed the man's countenance.

But she realised that, while she had J. Winthrop Stukes on his own, it was a perfect opportunity to get her investigation under way.

"I didn't see you at Mimsy La Pim's jazzjigger the other night . . . I'm sorry, I don't know what I should call you . . . J?"

"Winthrop. Everyone calls me Winthrop. Mention Winthrop to anyone in Hollywood and they'll know it's me you're talking about."

"Tickey-Tockey. Winthrop it is. As I say, I didn't see you at Mimsy's."

"Million other people you probably didn't see. Hollywood parties are like that. But I was there. Never miss a showbiz bash, me."

"Did you actually clap your peepers on Mimsy?"

"No, but that's not so odd. Same reason I didn't see you."

"But you sure she was actually there?"

"Stake my life on it. In fact, I was chatting to a couple of actors who're working with Toni Frangipani on *The Sheik of the Sahara*. They'd just been having a chinwag with young Mimsy. Said her agent had tried to get her the female lead in the movie, but no dice."

"Oh?"

"I'm afraid Mimsy La Pim's getting to that awkward age for an *ingénue*. She's a bit gnarled now to play the innocent, and Hollywood has a very efficient garbage chute for actresses who get too gnarled."

"But some of them still manage to keep a poker in the flames." Twinks gestured towards the set, where

107

Zelda Finch, still paralysed by a fear of snakes, was being teutonically bullied by her husband.

"Yes, but do you think she'd still be in work if she wasn't sleeping with the director? You heard of the casting couch, young lady?"

"Is it some kind of amenity for people who wish to fly-fish from a sedentary position?" Twinks asked in her mother's tones.

"No. It's the means by which most of the female parts in Hollywood are cast. Women sleep with the director — or, in Zelda's case, actually go a step further and marry the monster." Another exasperated "*Gott in Himmel!*" resounded from the set in front of them. "Though, with her," Stukes went on, "I don't see the marriage lasting very long. And when that goes down the pan, I think Zelda Finch's career could go with it."

"If we could pongle back to Mimsy La Pim for a momentette, Winthrop . . .?"

"Of course, my dear young lady."

"Do you have any thoughts about the identity of the stenchers who've kidnapped her?"

"Hmm." The veteran actor was contemplative for a moment. "Well, of course, she does mix with some fairly unsavoury types. Her current — what shall I say? Protector? — Well, he's up to his collar stud in organised crime. So it could be the work of some of his enemies . . . or, on the other hand, if he was starting to tire of Miss La Pim's charms he might have set the kidnap up himself."

"You're saying you think it's a Mafia job?"

"Could certainly be." Stukes rubbed his chin reflectively. "On the other hand, in cases like this, which often get blamed on organised crime, I think it's much more likely to be something closer up and more personal."

"Sorry, not on the same page?"

"Personal jealousy is a much more likely motive."

"Whose jealousy?"

"Mimsy La Pim's career may be on the skids now, but when she arrived in Hollywood she was everyone's dish of the day. Which meant her youthful innocence elbowed out someone else whose youthful innocence was beginning to show a few cracks. Women's jealousies last a long time, you know."

As he spoke, he gestured to the set, where stood an actress uncertain whether she was more scared by her crown of snakes or her husband.

"You mean that Zelda . . .?"

Twinks got no further as Hank Urchief came bustling up to them, glowing with confidence. "Well, I've fixed it!" he announced.

"Fixed what?" asked Twinks.

"Got you a bigger part, doll. Just had a word with the writer and persuaded him it was a good idea that Helen of Troy gets snatched by the Minotaur. That's why Theseus goes into the labyrinth: to rescue you just before the Minotaur eats you."

"And is that what's going to happen?"

"Sure thing, babe. It's a done deal. Writers don't argue with stars, you know."

Twinks looked down towards the two men on folding canvas chairs. Paul Uckliss-Hack was tearing his hair out, communicating the latest script change to Gervase Blunkett-Plunkett. As the professor took in the full enormity of what had happened, he started to pull his hair out too.

CHAPTER
TWELVE

Blotto Investigates

No one of Blotto's acquaintance actually worked, if you don't count servants and solicitors and people like that (and men of his breeding never did count servants and solicitors and people like that). So when he woke the following morning at the Hollywood Hotel and discovered that his sister was already on set filming as Helen of Troy in *The Trojan Horse*, he felt rather at a loss.

Of course, that didn't stop him from going down to the dining room to have breakfast. It wasn't like an English breakfast, though. The Americans really did have some strange ideas. Who would want to drink orange juice at that time in the morning? And why in the name of Denzil didn't cooks in America know that bacon should be served pink and slippery, not purple and crispy? In fact, the only thing his breakfast at the Hollywood Hotel had in common with the one he'd normally have at Tawcester Towers was that it was huge.

As he crunched up the last piece of cremated bacon and wiped the egg up off his plate with some rock-hard quoit called a bagel, he wondered how he was going to spend the day. The attraction of playing with his clockwork jumping frog seemed to have palled a bit. In a strange place without Twinks around . . . what could a boddo do? The feeling of being at a loss returned to him.

That was until he remembered he had a quest. Yes, of course, the day before he had decided to devote the rest of his life to finding Mimsy La Pim. How could he have forgotten something as important as that?

Toad in the hole, he reminded himself, he was going to be like Sir Gally . . . thing. Some half-remembered lines he'd heard from a beak at Eton drifted into his consciousness.

"My strength is as the strength of ten
Because my heart is pure . . ."

Yes, that's bong on the nose, he thought. Mind you, my strength won't be as the strength of ten, it'll be as the strength of a hundred. My heart's going to be as spoffing pure as . . . well, as spoffing pure as a heart can get. Like a knight of yore . . . though he was never quite sure what "yore" was . . . or when it was. And what was it Arthur's boddoes were always questing for, after a healthy breakfast at the Round Table . . .? Oh yes, the Holy Gruel. From now on, finding Mimsy La Pim was going to be Blotto's Holy Gruel.

How to do it, though? What should be his first step? He wished Twinks was there to ask. She'd know. She always knew guff like that. (Had Twinks been there, she would have been able to inform him that the lines which had emerged dimly into his mind through the fogs of adolescence had been written by Alfred Lord Tennyson. But she wasn't there, so Blotto remained, as he had for much of his life, uninformed.)

Blotto was still turning over in his mind the intractable question of what he should do next when he got back to his suite. Just as he entered, the telephone rang. He answered it.

"Ratteley-Baa-Baa!" Even if the voice hadn't identified the caller as Ponky Larreighffriebollaux, what he said would have done.

"Ritteley-Boo-Boo!" Blotto responded instinctively.

They galloped through the bits about fruitbats, suspenders, hippos and boot blackeners before the ritual's traditional end.

"Ra-ra!" said Ponky.

"Ra-ra-ra!" said Blotto.

"Listen, Blotto me old ship's biscuit, I've thought of a rather beezer way of spending the day."

"And what's that, Ponky me old snaffle bit?"

"I thought we could take out a cricket bat and ball to some park and just, you know, biffing it about a bit, like we used to do, you know, at prep school, even before we went to Eton. What do you say?"

Blotto couldn't deny he was tempted. The number of days he and Ponky had spent, biffing it about a bit with cricket bat and ball were beyond number. And each one had brought the warm glow of time well spent. But that was before he had a Quest, before he had dedicated himself to finding his Holy Gruel. So he said, "No."

The reply was so unexpected that it was a moment before Ponky could recover the power of speech.

"Is this your idea of a joke, Blotto? Are you jiggling my kneecap?"

"No," came the reply. "I cannot waste a day like that."

" 'Waste'?"

"Yes. 'Waste'."

"Why not?"

"Because", Blotto replied seriously, "I have a higher calling."

"A higher calling than cricket?" asked his friend.

"Yes."

"Well, tiddle my pom," said Ponky Larreighffriebollaux incredulously.

Blotto scoured his brain for leads in his investigation. It didn't take long. One of the great beauties of Blotto's brain, unlike that of most people, was that it was uncluttered by superfluous thought.

The one memory he could cling on to — in fact, the only lead he had in the case — was his sister's suggestion that there might be an Italian connection to the kidnapping.

So Blotto sauntered down to the hotel foyer and asked at the reception desk, "Do you know how I'd get in touch with the Mafia?"

The man he asked immediately ducked down behind the counter, as if in anticipation of machine-gun fire, and it took a while before he could be coaxed back into an upright posture. Blotto repeated his question.

"No, no, no," the man gabbled, "we have nothing to do with the Mafia at the Hollywood Hotel! There may be other hospitality businesses here in LA that pay protection money and host Mafia conferences, but you won't find any of that stuff going on here!"

"I wasn't suggesting that you were in the pay of the stenchers," Blotto reassured, "I just wondered what's the easiest way to get in touch with them."

The receptionist looked around the foyer and noticed the two Mediterranean types who had last been seen at Mimsy La Pim's party.

"I think you've found it," he told Blotto. "If you ask in a few more places the easiest way to get in touch with the Mafia, you'll get in touch with them, sure as eggs is eggs."

"Tickey-Tockey," said Blotto.

So he decided he might have an Italian lunch.

The restaurant on Hollywood Boulevard was called Giorgio's, and as soon as the waiter offered him the menu, Blotto repeated the question he had put to the hotel receptionist. "Do you know how I can get in touch with the Mafia?"

The reaction he got was not dissimilar. Panic came into the man's dark eyes. His moustache, which when Blotto entered the restaurant had been ripe for twirling, now drooped like the wattles of an apologetic bloodhound. Wordlessly, menu still in hand, the waiter dashed to the back of the room, picked up a telephone and burst into a panicked flurry of Italian with a range of gestures that suggested he might have a future in silent movies.

The moment he put the phone down, he quickly regained his composure. His moustache perked up and he went into Take Two of his greeting-a-new-customer routine. "Gooda afternoon, sir," he said. "Here issa the menu. Could I get you a drinka while you choose your luncha?"

Blotto hadn't thought whether he wanted a drink or not, but now the suggestion had been planted in the fertile vacancy of his brain, he realised what a good idea it was. "You don't by any chance do a buzzbanger of a cocktail called a St Louis Steamhammer, do you?"

The waiter smiled and said that indeed they did. In fact, their barman was renowned throughout Hollywood for the quality of his St Louis Steamhammers.

With a small bow the waiter receded, leaving his customer to study the menu. All panic had left the Italian's face. Whatever anxieties he may have had a few moments earlier seemed to have been allayed completely by what had been said on the telephone. He wore the complacent look of a man who knew that, whatever problems might arise, somebody else was going to sort them out.

Blotto, meanwhile, consulted the menu. It was not a very rewarding experience. He knew he was in an Italian restaurant, but he thought printing the menu in Italian was taking the whole concept far too far.

Needless to say, he didn't speak Italian. He thought that learning their languages was kowtowing to foreigners in a manner which was beyond the barbed wire. If communication was required — as he knew it might be in extreme circumstances — then it was down to them to learn English. It wasn't difficult. Even Blotto, who didn't have an unrealistic assessment of his intellectual prowess, had mastered the basics by the time he was five. Why on earth did people who were British go through what Blotto could avouch, from his years of French and Latin lessons at Eton, was the much more laborious process of learning foreign languages? Some perversities he would never understand.

Now it goes without saying that someone who'd grown up as Devereux Lyminster, scion of the noble house of Tawcester, had never before encountered Italian cooking. Like all people of his breeding, he had started out with nursery food and never moved far away from it. He'd been fed the same food at Eton, Tawcester Towers and other aristocratic households, and in the London restaurants and gentlemen's clubs he frequented. He'd certainly never eaten pasta.

But, narrow though his own mind actually was, Blotto liked to think of himself as a broad-minded boddo. So he was prepared to give this Italian menu a chance. He was quickly disappointed, however, by the very first word he encountered.

"Antipasto". His knowledge of foreign languages may have been limited, but even he could work out what that meant. "Anti", he knew, was "against". And, knowing foreigners' predilection for slapping gratuitous 'a's and 'o's on to the ends of perfectly workable English words, "pasto" must mean "past". So this restaurant he was in was actually "against the past", a sentiment that didn't sit well with someone whose family could be traced back to the Norman Conquest, and who rather regretted the abolition of the feudal system.

Blotto might have encountered further enormities in the menu had his attention not been diverted by the arrival of the waiter with his St Louis Steamhammer. Served in a tall glass with a long straw and maraschino cherry, its wonderful appearance diverted his mind from the inadequacies of Italian cuisine — a word he would not have recognised. Nor, indeed, would he have recognised *cucina*, which might have been more appropriate in the circumstances.

Blotto raised the straw to his lips, anticipating the tectonic shift of brain layers that the drink customarily induced. He took a long, hard slurp.

Great galumphing goatherds! I've never felt an impact like that from any previous St Louis Steamhammers! The barman at this Italian restaurant deserves some kind of international award . . .

These were the last thoughts that went through Blotto's mind before he slipped into oblivion. Distracted by the arrival of his drink, he had not been aware of the contemporaneous arrival through the restaurant door of the two Mediterranean types he'd failed to notice on the S.S. *Regal*, at Mimsy La Pim's party or in the foyer of the Hollywood Hotel. Nor had he been aware of the lead-filled sock with which one of them had struck him over the back of the neck.

As a result, he was also unaware of being bundled out of the restaurant into the back of a black limousine.

118

And unaware of being driven at breakneck speed along the streets of Los Angeles.

In fact, the next thing he was aware of was waking up with a splitting headache, with his arms tied to a chair and facing Lenny "The Skull" Orvieto.

Blotto had to admit, though, that the receptionist at the Hollywood Hotel had had a point. The easiest way of getting in touch with the Mafia was to ask *how* to get in touch with them.

CHAPTER
THIRTEEN

Lenny "The Skull" Orvieto

It wasn't difficult to work out how Lenny Orvieto had got his nickname. His head was hairless and there seemed to be only a paper-thin layer of skin covering his cranium. His nose was short and his dark eyes lurked in hollow sockets like evil monsters in caves.

Orvieto was dressed in a light brown suit with a pale yellow pinstripe. On the front of his grey silk shirt a blue-patterned tie was affixed by a diamond pin. The effect was dapper to the point of being dandyish and, though he couldn't see the man's feet, Blotto knew they would be wearing spats.

Through the pain in his head, he managed to take in the room in which he found himself. It was windowless, painted pale green and smartly furnished. Having been brought up in Tawcester Towers, Blotto didn't know that being an interior designer was a profession, but someone more *au fait* with the ways of the world would have recognised one had been at work in this room. There was a lot of gilt, on the chairs, on the desk behind which "The Skull" sat, and on the ornate frame of the large mirror behind him. This reflected the perfect dome of his hairless head, as well as his two Mediterranean abductors, who were seated behind Blotto.

On the gilt desk lay a snub-nosed automatic pistol.

The boss's voice had no trace of an Italian accent. He spoke very softly and soothingly, which somehow made him more menacing. If a viper could speak it would have sounded very much like Lenny "The Skull" Orvieto.

"So . . ." he said to the still-dazed Blotto, "I hear you want to get in touch with the Mafia?"

"Good ticket," said Blotto blearily.

"I do not like it."

"Do not like what?"

"The use of the term 'Mafia' in relation to myself."

"Oh?"

"I prefer the expression 'Cosa Nostra'."

"Tickey-Tockey." Blotto nodded sagely, then asked, "What does that mean?"

"In Italian? It means 'our thing'."

"And what actually is your 'thing'?"

"The Cosa Nostra", Lenny replied smoothly, "is a charitable organisation set up to look to the welfare of immigrants from Italy when they arrive in the United States."

Blotto could have sworn he heard stifled snorts of laughter from the two Mediterranean heavies behind him.

"And you look after these Italian boddoes by coffinating people who threaten them?" he asked in a combative manner.

At this suggestion, the thin skin on the bald man's forehead wrinkled as if in pain. "Please . . . where do you get these ideas from? The Cosa Nostra is a peaceful institution, financed solely by charitable donations. We are not associated with any criminal activity."

Blotto searched Orvieto's expression for signs of irony, but could see none. "So," he asked, "the Cosa Nostra is different hand of bananas from the Mafia?"

"Very much so. That is why I was hurt when you used the expression 'Mafia'."

Blotto was abjectly apologetic. "Sorry, I really do seem to have got the wrong end of the sink plunger here."

"I think you have."

"So the Cosa Nostra doesn't demand protection money from poor greengages trying to run legitimate businesses?"

"No."

"It doesn't control the drugs trade?"

"No."

"And it doesn't go around with machine-guns coffinating people who disagree with it?"

"No." Lenny "The Skull" Orvieto laughed at the incongruity of the suggestion. Behind him Blotto heard echoing laughter from the two thugs. "As I say, we are a peaceful organisation. We deplore the use of violence in any situation."

"Well, I'll be jugged like a hare . . ." Still suffering from the blow to the back of his head, Blotto's brain was working even slower than usual, but he did manage to spot an inconsistency in what the man opposite had just said. "Just a hiccup, though . . . If you deplore the use of violence in any situation," Blotto began slowly, "why did your blunder-thugs biff me over the bonce with a loaded sock?"

"Ah." Lenny spread his hands wide in a gesture of apology. "I'm afraid Giovanni and Giuseppe do sometimes get a little carried away and forget the principles of peace and altruism that are the basis of our Cosa Nostra beliefs."

"Tickey-Tockey," said Blotto.

"It is because of their upbringing, you see. Giovanni and Giuseppe grew up in extreme poverty in Sicily. They were orphaned at a very early age. When they first came to America, they got in with some bad company, they were set on a path of violence and criminality. Yes, I will use the word . . . they became embroiled with the 'Mafia'. But for the charitable efforts of the Cosa Nostra in making them realise their social responsibilities, they might irredeemably have gone to the bad. But fortunately the Cosa Nostra turned their lives around. They renounced criminality and violence and undertook to devote their lives to helping others. Only very occasionally, like this afternoon, do they backslide and hit people over the head with loaded socks. Of course they are very sorry and wish to apologise to you for that unpardonable lapse in behaviour. Don't you, Giovanni and Giuseppe?"

Apologies were growled out behind Blotto.

"I fully understand," he said. "Of course, I have no experience of growing up in poverty, but I can readily believe that it could cock a boddo's eye more than

123

somewhat. So I readily forgive the chaps' lapse with the loaded sock."

"Excellent."

"One other thingette, though, Mr Orvieto . . ."

"Mm?"

"If you're such a peaceful organisation, why have you tied me to the chair?"

The Italian spread his arms wide in a gesture of helplessness. "We are a peaceful organisation, but we don't know where *you* fit into the hierarchy of evil, do we? You might be armed and dangerous. We tie you to the chair only for our own protection."

This seemed such a reasonable reply that Blotto accorded it another "Tickey-Tockey".

A thin smile cut across Lenny "The Skull" Orvieto's cavernous face. "Now what we haven't established, Mr Devereux, is why you wanted to contact the Mafia."

Blotto chuckled innocently. "And why I ended up talking to the Cosa Nostra instead."

"Exactly."

"Well, it's rather a jiggling tale and probably not something where you can give me much of a jockey-up, but have you heard of a breathsapper of an actress called Mimsy La Pim?"

Lenny "The Skull" Orvieto appeared to be riffling through the card-index of his brain before conceding that he thought he'd heard the name. Which, if Blotto had known what Hank Urchief had told Twinks about the relationship between the two, he would have recognised as a very skilful bit of acting.

"Some fumacious stenchers have kidnapped her."

"Is that so?" said Lenny, giving a very good impression of surprise.

"And I thought you were the kind of boddoes who might have a mousesqueak of an idea where she might be found." In response to Orvieto's wide-handed gesture of helplessness, Blotto went on, "Of course, that was when I thought you were the kind of lumps of toadspawn who belonged to the Mafia. Now I know that you represent a charitable organisation like the Cosa Nostra . . . well, obviously I realise I'm shinnying up the wrong drainpipe."

Lenny "The Skull" Orvieto shrugged sympathetically. "If I could help you, then of course I would."

"I'm sure you would. I can tell, just by looking at you, that you're a Grade A foundation stone."

Lenny nodded gratitude for the compliment. "I guess you need to find some real Mafia people."

"Good ticket. Any idea how I might do that?"

The shrug that greeted him made Blotto realise the incongruity of his question. How could someone who ran a charitable organisation like the Cosa Nostra have any contact with a crime syndicate like the Mafia? In fact, it was insulting to his host even to raise the suggestion.

Blotto's profuse apologies were interrupted by Orvieto. "Don't worry about it. We all make mistakes. And listen, if you do manage to find this Mimsy La Pim, let me know about it. She sounds, from all accounts, like a real classy broad. I wouldn't want anything unpleasant to happen to her."

"Tickey-Tockey," said Blotto. "I think perhaps I ought to be pongling off now."

"Of course." Lenny "The Skull" Orvieto gestured to Giovanni and Giuseppe, who came forward to untie the ropes that tied their prisoner's arms to his chair. Freed, Blotto rose, as if to take his leave, but then lingered for a moment.

"Is there something else I can do for you?" asked Lenny "The Skull" Orvieto.

"No," Blotto replied. "But, by Wilberforce, there's something I can do for you." He reached into the pocket of his jacket and produced five crisp ten-dollar bills. As he handed them across, he said, "You told me your only support was charitable donations. I'd like you to have this, to further the activities of the Cosa Nostra."

"That's very kind," said Orvieto. "You're a real gentleman."

"Keep up the good work," said Blotto.

Then he allowed Giovanni and Giuseppe to blindfold him, lead him out of the room and back into their car. They left him in the middle of Hollywood Boulevard without the beginning of an idea where Lenny "The Skull" Orvieto's headquarters were.

CHAPTER
FOURTEEN

A Surfeit of Amorous Swains

Twinks was ambivalent about her new role as a star of the silver screen. The work was not onerous. She just had to stand in front of the camera being alternately bullied and cajoled by Gottfried von Klappentrappen to look beautiful, something which came naturally to her, anyway.

She soon discovered that the chief drawback to being a film actress was that she spent so little time in front of the camera. Though Helen of Troy had been shoehorned into more scenes than history or myth had ever offered her before (causing the classical adviser Professor Gervase Blunkett-Plunkett to pull out even more of his remaining hair), there were acres of time spent just hanging around the set. Twinks, active by nature, had a very low boredom threshold, and the pleasures of film-making soon began to pall. She picked up the translation of Sun Tzu's *The Art of War* into Gujarati which she had started on the S.S. *Regal* to work on during her long breaks from shooting, but her heart wasn't really in it.

On the other hand, she was, for the first time in her life, experiencing the novel sensation of being paid.

Someone who had been brought up like Honoria Lyminster had never been involved with something as demeaning as work. She told herself she'd only taken on the part of Helen of Troy as a means of investigating Mimsy La Pim's kidnapping, but the fact remained that Hank Urchief's agent Lefty Switzer (who, Hank had insisted, should act on her behalf) had negotiated a very advantageous deal for her services, so she was being paid a huge amount of money for hanging around on a film set.

For the first time, for a very short moment, Twinks contemplated having a career beyond amateur sleuthing. A couple of years in Hollywood, being paid at the rate she was for Helen of Troy, and she'd be able to sort out the Tawcester Towers plumbing single-handed. That was a much more attractive prospect than marrying a Texas oil millionaire — certainly if they were all as taciturn as Wilbur T. Cottonpick.

The idea of financial self-sufficiency also appealed to the strong independent streak in Twinks. She didn't want her financial well-being to be controlled by her family or, even worse, by a husband.

Yes, maybe the acting lark did have a lot to be said for it.

Being the new star on the block, though, brought with it a tiresome number of commitments away from the studio. The *Trojan Horse* publicity machine at Humungous Studios, in collaboration with her new agent Lefty Switzer, kept demanding that she make personal appearances at the smartest venues. Wherever

Twinks went, flashlights popped and blazed. Her picture was all over the Hollywood papers. Heddan Schoulders and her coven of lesser gossip columnists kept printing new (and completely erroneous) insights into her character and private life.

Hollywood, starved of real history, loved her aristocratic background, and it soon became common knowledge that Honoria Lyminster was in truth the illegitimate daughter of George V. Much mileage was gained from the difference in her background from that of Hank Urchief, who had, of course, been brought up on a turkey farm in Minnesota, because the gossip columns assumed — to Twinks's considerable annoyance — that she and Hank were enjoying an extraordinarily steamy love affair. It took her a while to realise, when interviewed by the press, that to say she and the actor were "just good friends" was Hollywood code for a rampantly physical relationship. She decided saying nothing might be a way of avoiding the inferences they picked up, but that only convinced the scribblers that she was hiding something — and gave them carte blanche to make up whatever fictions they chose.

Another part of Twinks's new role in life was an obligatory attendance at parties. If she had thought Mimsy La Pim's was a one-off occasion, it soon became clear that there was at least one event on the same scale or bigger every night in Hollywood.

And The Trojan Horse's publicity team insisted that the film world's newest star couldn't escape attending as many of them as possible.

★ ★ ★

It was at the end of her third day of extravagantly paid time-wasting on the film set that Twinks was dragooned into attending a party at Toni Frangipani's house. She had no particular desire to see the self-regarding lothario again, but the bullies in Humungous Studios' publicity department said it was her contractual obligation to be there. There were lots of things they said she had a contractual obligation to do and, since she had never seen the contract that Lefty Switzer had signed on her behalf, it was hard for her to argue.

So she went to the party with a minder from the Humungous Studios publicity department to check she didn't sneak off too early. And she went with bad grace. Which was unusual for Twinks. Like her brother, her emotional barometer was set permanently to "sunny", but that evening storm clouds threatened. Maybe the unfamiliar experience of three days' actual work had tired her. Never before had she been forced to experience how the other half lived.

Twinks was not the kind of girl who would have worried about going to a party where she didn't know anyone. Self-possession in any environment was an essential product of her upbringing.

Anyway, though she knew few people at Toni Frangipani's, there seemed to be plenty who knew her. Even in such a short time, the news of *The Trojan Horse*'s new Helen of Troy had spread to every level of Hollywood society. Nothing as formal as an introduction was required by these brash Angelenos, who all seemed to regard Honoria Lyminster as their personal property. Apparently, everyone was entitled to a piece of her, and her every move was monitored. Heddan Schoulders and her lesser acolytes lurked with pencils poised over notebooks, waiting for some new tiny foundation of detail on which they could erect another edifice of lies.

Toni Frangipani's house was even bigger than Mimsy La Pim's, and in his case the architectural style being bastardised was that of the medieval castle. Twinks, who had spent her entire life in authentic medieval castles, was unimpressed by its splendours. The coats of armour standing in every corner were clearly replicas, and the faces staring from the frames in the Long Gallery were from Central Casting. She felt a twinge of patrician pity for people who had grown up in a land with no history.

Nor was she impressed by a further encounter with the house's owner. Toni seemed to regard the fact that she had come to his party as proof she had seen the error of her ways and was as susceptible to his charms as every other woman in the movie-going universe. The first words he said to her were, "It issa up to you. Either we go to the beddaroom now — my guests do notta need my permanenta presence — or we waita till they have gonna and you staya here the nighta. The choicea is yours."

"My choice," responded Twinks, with the iciness that can only come from generations of maltreating serfs, "is that you stop behaving like a peacock posturing in a mirror. If you think I want to spend more time than I have to with a lump of toadspawn like you, then I'm sure I can find you the address of a suitable bonkers-doctor. I believe that profession is one that's thriving in Hollywood. In case you haven't already twigged my drift — and I don't get the impression that you're a whale among intellects — then my choice is that I never see your greasy Italian face or hear your squeaky Italian voice again. Are we on the same page now?"

An expression of shocked affront was not one that, in the course of his career, Toni Frangipani had ever been required to assume before. Indeed, his silent movies had only demanded two expressions: heroic nobility when he set off into battle and snarling contempt when he was alone with a woman. His mouth opened and closed in astonishment, but no words came. Then he quickly moved away to find a more acquiescent member of the opposite sex (not a difficult thing to do in Hollywood).

Hank Urchief who, along with most of the Hollywood A-list, had witnessed the encounter, smiled a smile of self-congratulation. In the notebooks of Heddan Schoulders and her lesser acolytes, notes were written at a rate of knots. What Twinks was giving them was pure gold dust.

Hardly had Toni Frangipani beaten his retreat than Twinks was accosted by another aspirant for her favours. Their argument over Medusa's circlet of snakes had brought a coolness into the director's relationship with his latest wife. He was also hearing ever stronger rumours on *The Trojan Horse* set that Zelda's fidelity might be open to question. If he found them to be true, and if he could identify the culprit, which shouldn't be too difficult amid the swirling gossip of Hollywood, then his revenge would be swift and terrible.

In the meantime, it made sense for him to start looking elsewhere for female companionship. He was not unaware of the photographic coverage and column inches that his new Helen of Troy, Honoria Lyminster, was getting, and besides, for a director of von Klappentrappen's status, an emotional entanglement with his latest leading lady was *de rigueur*.

Though the plain — very plain — fact was obvious to everyone who encountered him, and though he spent his life surrounded by some of the most beautiful people on the planet, it still hadn't occurred to Gottfried von Klappentrappen that he was unattractive. His power and influence in Hollywood had not, up until then, allowed many women in the movie world to resist his advances. But then, of course, he hadn't tried coming on to Twinks before.

"Hi, sugar lump," he said, bouncing up to her like a rubber ball.

Honoria Lyminster bridled. "I am not a spoffing sugar lump!"

"You sure are sweet enough to be. And if you and I got together, things could be even sweeter."

"That I doubt," said Twinks, only showing the tip of the iceberg but making it clear there was a whole lot more underneath.

"What say," suggested the von Klappentrappen, impervious to the Antarctic blast being directed at him, "we go off for a spot of dinner, *a deux* as the French put it and" — he chuckled teutonically — "see how the evening ends up."

"We don't need to go through all that clangdumble," came the spirited response. "I can tell you exactly how the evening ends up for us . . . because it's ending zappity-ping right now! When I want to spend my free time with a groping slimeball who doesn't even make it to zero on the charm-scale, I'll be sure to let you know!"

Twinks moved away from Gottfried von Klapp-entrappen, who was mouthing silently in exactly the same way Toni Frangipani had.

Hank Urchief's self-congratulatory smile was even broader this time. Meanwhile, scribbling away like mad, Heddan Schoulders and her lesser acolytes could not believe their good fortune.

It was perhaps inevitable that, as Twinks reached for a glass of champagne from the tray of a passing waiter, it should be picked up and handed to her by another amorous swain. Wilbur T. Cottonpick, who was dressed in a spangly suit that made him look like a bullock wrapped in tinsel.

"Hi," he said. Then, being, as she had discovered, a man of three words, he let his actions substitute verbal blandishments. Putting his arms around her, the Texas oil millionaire reached his lips towards hers.

Twinks recoiled as if she'd been electrocuted. "Are you attempting to kiss me?" she demanded.

"Yup," said Wilbur T. Cottonpick.

134

"And has it occurred to your minuscule pea of a brain that I might not want your fumacious lips on mine?"

"Nope," said Wilbur T. Cottonpick.

"Well, you spavined clip-clop, will you infiltrate into your granite cranium the notion that I do not like being touched by men with the manners of mismanaged mules!" The plan, which she had only vaguely contemplated in the first place, of saving the Tawcester Towers plumbing by marrying a Texas oil millionaire, was now very nearly out of the window. If Wilbur T. Cottonpick had ever been in the frame for that role, he certainly wouldn't be after her next words. "And the idea that I, Honoria Lyminster, would give a tinker's tuppence about someone as underbred as you would raise a laugh from an Easter Island statue!"

As with the two previous recipients of Twinks's scorn, Wilbur T. Cottonpick's mouth moved up and down in shock, but was unable to pronounce a single one of his three words.

The scribbling speed of Heddan Schoulders and her lesser acolytes was now rivalling the Flying Scotsman. Hank Urchief smiled at them confidently as he sashayed across to join Twinks.

"Nice work," he said.

She looked at him in puzzlement. "I'm sorry? I haven't a mouse-squeak of an idea what you're talking about."

"I was listening when you saw off those three."

"I was brought up by my Mater to believe it was bad manners to eavesdrop on other people's conversations. That kind of behaviour is totally beyond the barrier."

"Hey, Twinks, cool it. We're in Hollywood now. No one gets too fussed about protocol out here."

"So I observe," she said acidly.

"Take eavesdropping away and the whole system would grind to a halt. It's at the centre of the whole movie publicity machine."

"That still doesn't make it *polite*." Twinks caught her mother's intonations perfectly.

The star let out a relaxed chuckle. "I like a woman who has standards."

"Glad to hear it. I wouldn't think you find that many of them out here."

"And I like a woman who has spirit. Has anyone ever told you, Twinks, that you look beautiful when you're angry?"

"Nobody of my acquaintance would have had the brazen effrontery to say anything of the kind. My Mater also brought me up to believe that making personal remarks is the behaviour of the guttersnipe."

"Bully for her. She sounds like one tough old bird. And she certainly produced one beautiful daughter; beautiful when she's angry and beautiful when she ain't. Anyhow, I like what you said to Toni and Gottie and Wilbur."

"Why?"

"Hell, because you put all three of the dumb clucks in their place."

Twinks shrugged.

"What's more," Hank Urchief continued with a sly smile, "I kinda liked it from my point of view."

The smallest wrinkle of puzzlement crossed her perfect brow. "Why?"

"Well, you just gave the bum's rush to one of the sexiest men in Hollywood, one of the most powerful men in Hollywood and one of the richest men in Hollywood. There aren't many people out here who'd dare to do that."

The perfect shoulders shrugged again. "It's no icing off my birthday cake. I just speak as I find."

"That's a very rare thing out here in Hollywood."

"Why?"

"Because getting on the wrong side of powerful people is a pretty sure way of digging a great big grave for your career."

"And why should that worry me?"

"Hell, that kind of stuff worries everyone."

"Not me," said Twinks, speaking no more than the truth. "If doing what I've been doing for the last three days is 'having a career', then it's as much fun as milking frogs."

"Hey, but you're the hottest stuff Hollywood's seen for a long time."

"Don't talk such toffee," said Twinks.

"You've just realised the dream of every girl. You're playing Helen of Troy in Gottfried von Klappentrappen's *The Trojan Horse*. What's more, you're playing opposite *me*. That's about as good as it gets for an American girl."

Twinks was about to say that, compared to English girls, American girls were very easily satisfied, when Hank Urchief went on, "Besides, you got more than that. You're my girl."

"I beg your pardon?"

"You're my girl. That's why I was so pleased when I heard you cut the other three off at the knees. That was you saying, 'Get lost, losers! The broad you're dealing with here is Hank Urchief's girl.'"

"You think that's why I — to use your colourful but indelicate phrase — 'cut them off at the knees'? Because you have some kind of ownership deal on me?"

"Sure thing, babe."

"Well, Mr Urchief, you've got things about as wrong as the man who thought he'd picked up a cooked prawn and put a live scorpion in his mouth. I am not *anyone's* girl. I am a person, not something that can be sold by the pound like fresh fish! Nobody owns me! You can own a dog, you can own a racehorse, maybe out here in Hollywood there *are* people you can own, but I, Honoria Lyminster, am not one of them! I have no intention of spending my life dangling on some man's charm bracelet. And if you thought I was going to be impressed by your so-called celebrity, then the women you usually spend your time with must all be soft-yolked voidbrains. You, Mr Urchief, as it says all over your publicity, were brought up on a turkey farm in Minnesota. Out here that may be a tick on your homework, but where I come from, to admit to such a background would be regarded as irredeemably *common*!"

Though he didn't know the full appalling implications back in England of her final word, Hank Urchief got the gist from Twinks's intonation. He looked humbled and chastened, then he noticed that her raised voice had attracted considerable attention to their exchange, and that the top names in Hollywood stood, gaping, in a circle around them.

"So, Mr Urchief," said Twinks from the very pinnacle of her hauteur, "I have only one more thing to say." She turned to face her victim as she pronounced the words: "Snubbins to you!"

The phrase may have been unfamiliar to the Californian crowd, but there was no mistaking its meaning. A communal shocked intake of breath was followed by a communal silence as Twinks found her Humungous Studios publicity minder and, in that voice of her mother's that brooked no argument, demanded a car to take her back to the Hollywood Hotel immediately.

The pencils of Heddan Schoulders and her lesser acolytes could hardly be seen, so fast were they moving across the paper of their notebooks.

CHAPTER
FIFTEEN

Heddan Tales

BRIT BARONETTE HUMILIATES
HOLLYWOOD HUNKS!!!

Yes, once again your friendly dirt-disher, your hack on the inside track, your bulletin buddy Heddan Schoulders was right on the hot spotteroonie when what happens happens. And boy, did it happen at last night's party, given by sultry sheik Toni Frangipani! Hollywood's new sensation, important English import, the frock with the purtiest clock on the block, Honoria Lyminster, whose Helen of Troy has turned *The Trojan Horse* into a stamping stallion, has shown what it's like to be real royalty. Last night she put so-called Hollywood royalty in its place with a handful of lizard licks from her pretty little tongue.

First to put his incautious head on the block was her host, Toni Frangipani himself. If you believe his publicity, there's not a woman on the planet who wouldn't roll over like a poodle for oodles of canoodling with the Sheik of the Sahara. Toni only has to turn his smouldering eyes on some babe and the tottie instantly turns hottie. Toni flickers through more female fantasies than a centipede has socks. Uh-uh, not any more, I think we'll have to redraft his résumé! Last night, in front of all the Hollywood high-rollers, Lady Honoria Lyminster treated Mr Frangipani like an Italian waiter who'd just slopped the soup over her! Not content with wiping the floor with him, she wrung him out as well. Baroness Lyminster reduced Toni Frangipani from Hollywood stud to collar stud. Not so much a dressing-down as a stripping naked to his birthday suiteroonie. Wow, did she put a big pin in his balloon! It might just be that, through his Italian connections, the shook-up sheik and ultimate it-man may be looking for a hitman.

But that wasn't a full evening's work for our dangerous duchess. Next, she was propositioned by Teutonic tyrant, Gottie von Klappentrappen. Most movie models who'd just been cast in his latest crackerjack *The Trojan Horse* would be doing contortions to keep the right side of the movie maestro whose restless eye seems to be on the rove again. What's more, rumours of ructions with his latest wifie, superannuated siren Zelda Finch, mean the bouncing ball may once again be looking to bounce into other boudoirs. But after the words exchanged last night, one boudoir the Prussian playboy won't be bouncing into belongs to his new Helen of Troy. The flea she put in his ear was so big Gottie's gonna be deaf for months!

Some dishy dames might call it a day at that, but not our perky princess. Her next knuckle-up was with lip-zipping zillionaire Wilbur T. Cottonpick, who's got financial fingers in more pies than you see in a math test. But no amount of mazuma makes a match with our forthright filly. Cottonpick too was cut down to the size of a cricket.

But hey, I hear you saying, that kind of behaviour's bonzer if a broad's gotta boyfriend. And didn't you hear from this column — more reliable than Wells Fargo — that Honoria Lyminster was sharing snuggle-time with Minnesota Mightyman Hank Urchief? Well, if you'd heard what she said to him last night, you'd think the unthinkable — that your smear-supplier Heddan Schoulders had got something wrong! If I did, it's because my source of secrets on that scene was none other than Hank Urchief himself. I guess he, like a whole lotta men, was just bigging up his boudoir credentials.

So, four cinematic skirt-chasers brought down in one evening by one brave broaderoonie. And what do we dumped-on dames say about the destruction of those four egos by Queen Honoria of Lyminster? We say: "Good on ya, gal! Keep up the good work!"

CHAPTER
SIXTEEN

Kidnappers Beware!

Neither Blotto nor Twinks read the newspaper in which
Heddan Schoulders' daily column was published and
drooled over by everyone else in Hollywood. So they
weren't aware how Twinks's evening at Toni Frangipani's
had been chronicled. Nor were they aware of the
shockwaves the column had sent through the
film-making world. Four industry icons had been cut
down to size in a way that rarely happens in Hollywood
to people who are still in their pomp. (People whose
careers were on the slide were reckoned to be fair
game. Many stars of yesterday had had their
professional demise hastened by pillorying in the gossip
columns. It was too easy for the commentators, like
shooting fish in a barrel. But soon after, the
unfortunate former stars were treated to a worse fate
than vilification from the gossip columnists: total
silence from them. No coverage of any kind. The silent
telephone, the unreturned calls to agents and
producers. Total eclipse of career. Hollywood could be
a cruel place.)

So the incidents at Toni Frangipani's remained
undiscussed by the aristocratic siblings as they drank

room service cocktails in Blotto's suite at the Hollywood Hotel. He certainly had more important things on his mind. "I'm stuck up a chimney with a sweep's brush behind me, Twinks me old chammy leather. There don't seem to be any leads on Mimsy's kidnapping."

"And when you met Lenny Orvieto, you really didn't get a whiff that the Stilton was iffy?"

"No, he's a Grade A foundation stone. Kind of boddo one wouldn't hesitate to go into the jungle with. Runs this absolutely pukka charitable set-up to help out poor greengages from Italy when they first arrive in the States. It's called the Cosa Nostra."

"Is it?" asked Twinks, suspicion glinting in her azure eyes. "I understood that the Cosa Nostra was just another monicker for the Mafia."

"Wrong on all counts, my dear sis." It was rarely that Blotto had to put Twinks right on any matter of fact, and he found he was rather enjoying the experience. "Apparently, a lot of people plump for the wrong plum there. No, the Mafia's a nasty load of stenchers, into drugs, protection rackets and all that kind of rombooley. Whereas the Cosa Nostra just help people out — like the Good Samurai."

"I think you probably mean 'Samaritan'," his sister suggested.

"Possibly," Blotto conceded. "Anyway, the Cosa Nostra are definitely on the good side of the egg basket."

Twinks still didn't look convinced. "Blotto me old tin of tooth powder . . ." she began tentatively.

"What is it, Twinks me old needle and thread?" She was silent for a moment. "Come on, uncage the ferrets."

"Well," she continued diffidently, "I think maybe, Blotters, you should prepare yourself for the tidgy possibility that Lenny 'The Skull' Orvieto may not be all that he seems."

"What, you mean that in real life he's got hair?"

"No, that wasn't quite the pen I was pushing. Fact is, I happen to know that, whatever spaghetti he may be feeding you, he's actually an extremely vicious and violent Mafia boss."

"Well, I'll be battered like a pudding!" Blotto thought for a slow moment, then said, "Sorry, Twinks me old Bath Oliver, but I'm afraid I don't believe you."

"It's Jemima's very own truth!" his sister protested. "I was told by no less a person than Hank Urchief."

This did give Blotto pause. The one man whose heroism he had never doubted, whose word was his bond and who was no more capable of lying than George Washington after cutting down the rain forest, was Chaps Chapple. And the actor who played Chaps Chapple was Hank Urchief. So if he said something, it must be true.

"Tickey-Tockey, Twinks," he said slowly. "I think I'll have to recalibrate my binoculars as far as Lenny 'The Skull' Orvieto is concerned."

"I'm afraid you'd better, Blotters."

A rare flash of anger reddened her brother's usually serene countenance. "To think I believed the lump of toadspawn, and all the time he was just jiggling my kneecap."

"I'm afraid he was, Blotters."

"Well, nobody jiggles Devereux Lyminster's kneecap and gets away with it. I'll go back to Lenny Orvieto and grill him like a well-done steak. We have strong reason to believe there's a Mafia connection to Mimsy La Pim's kidnapping. If Lenny's the biggest Mafia boss in Hollywood, then he must be behind the crime. I'll confront him and demand to know why he wanted to do the vanishing trick on a sweet, innocent little sugar cube like Mimsy."

"Ye-es." Twinks hesitated. Though normally the most forthright of women, she never felt very happy about giving her brother bad news. But in this instance, it couldn't be avoided. "There was something else Hank told me about Lenny 'The Skull' Orvieto . . . something you might find a bit of a candle-snuffer . . ." She stopped.

"What was it? Now come on, Twinks, don't fiddle round the furniture. Tell me the worst."

Reluctantly his sister did as she was told. "To quote his own words, Hank Urchief described Mimsy La Pim as Lenny 'The Skull' Orvieto's 'current bit of skirt'."

"Ah," said Blotto. Then, hopefully. "I assume that doesn't mean she's something he wears?"

"No, it doesn't."

"I thought it probably didn't." He struggled to digest the new information. "This turns the decanter on its head a bit, doesn't it?"

"I'm afraid it does, Blotters."

146

"Yes."

Twinks allowed him a long silence to readjust to the new complexion that had just been put on things. Then she said softly, "There *is* one silver sixpence in the Christmas pudding, though, brother of mine."

"Is there?" asked Blotto dolorously. He was unable to see any mitigating streak of light in the unremitting gloom into which Twinks's words had cast him.

"Well, presumably, now you know this about Mimsy La Pim, you no longer feel you have to follow your quest to rescue her?"

"Puddledash!" cried Blotto. "The very opposite! I will redouble my efforts! My mission is clearer than ever! Now there are two evil monsters from whom I must save Mimsy La Pim! The one who has kidnapped her and also the one who has imposed his wicked will upon her innocence — in other words, Lenny 'The Skull' Orvieto! I, Devereux Lyminster, will rescue her from both those four-faced filchers. And I will succeed in my quest because my heart is pure — just like Sir Galleyproof."

"Galahad," said Twinks gently.

CHAPTER
SEVENTEEN

A New Helen of Troy?

The ego of the Hollywood male star is a force not to be underestimated. Though lording it through the waters of the film world like a killer whale, at the same time it's as sensitive as a neurotic sea anemone. Swelling itself up like a bullfrog's throat, it's just as easily deflated.

And Heddan Schoulders' report of Twinks's actions at Toni Frangipani's party had had a very deflating effect, not only on his ego but also on those of three other major players in Hollywood.

Men are not subtle creatures. Having suffered public humiliation at the hands of Twinks, all four injured parties demanded revenge.

For Gottfried von Klappentrappen the sense of grievance was twofold. Not only had his distended ego been publicly pricked by his new Helen of Troy, he also had worrying suspicions about the fidelity of his seventh wife.

On the set of *The Trojan Horse* the day Heddan Schoulders' column was published, the director brooded like a globular landmine, liable to explode if anyone encroached on his private space. Woe betide the

Greek soldier who got out of step or the Trojan one who poured his boiling oil from the ramparts too early that day. They got bawled out in a fine mixture of Californian and German.

Nor did his stars get much better treatment. Even without his other suspicions, Zelda Finch's ophidiophobia was really getting on his nerves, so much so that he couldn't see his seventh marriage lasting a lot longer. And Hank Urchief's laid-back cowboy casualness seemed by the hour to be increasingly unsuitable for a Greek hero. The star looked ill-at-ease slouching around in a breastplate and short tunic, and his bare legs seemed to be crying out to be covered by Chaps Chapple's chaps. Von Klappentrappen bawled him out too. Everyone in the studio suffered from their director's mood.

What made him particularly angry was the certainty that everyone around him knew more than he did. He was aware that a Hollywood film set has a communication system considerably speedier than the latest technology of telegraphs and transatlantic cables. And some off-camera sniggering suggested that most people on *The Trojan Horse* set could provide more details of his wife's indiscretions than he could. He had to find out more.

He had only one source from which to get his information — the source of the rumour about Zelda and the blond-haired young man at Mimsy La Pim's party. A source he now knew to be called Buza Cruz, though he couldn't put a face to the name as there were hundreds of pretty little starlets employed on a project the size of *The Trojan Horse*.

A few questions to the stage crew had her quickly identified, though, and at lunch break von Klappentrappen didn't turn to the gourmet food hamper he had supplied on set every day, but slummed it by going into the Humungous Studios commissary with the rest of the cast and crew.

Buza Cruz was sitting at a table with a gaggle of other starlets. For someone who, on screen, was only capable of looking as if she'd been turned to stone, she was remarkably animated. Clearly the leader of the gaggle, she led their giggling.

Which stopped abruptly as Gottfried von Klappentrappen approached the table. The sight of the director in the commissary was sufficiently unusual to ensure the silence continued. He pointed to Buza Cruz and said, "I want to talk to you. The rest — *raus!*" The gesture that accompanied the word made its meaning clear to those who didn't understand German, and the gaggle scattered in a flurry of excited whispers.

Von Klappentrappen sat opposite Buza Cruz, who tried hard to look her most seductive. She was a calculating little beast, who recognised that in Hollywood she was a commodity, and knew to the last cent the value of her looks and her body. Being singled out by the director could mean a lot of things, most of them good. He could be about to offer her a bigger part in *The Trojan Horse*. She might have caught his roving eye and be the target of his seductive intentions. Either scenario could do no harm to her career prospects.

But what he said took her by surprise. "You were at a party given by Mimsy La Pim last week."

She didn't deny it.

"My wife Zelda Finch was also present."

She didn't deny that either.

"Rumour round the set has it that you saw her go into one of the bedrooms with a young man."

Buza Cruz was silent. Gottfried von Klappentrappen was after information, and in her commodified world information, like everything else, had a price. Feeling empowered, she said, "Maybe I did, maybe I didn't."

"I would give a lot to know the identity of that young man."

"A lot? How much?" asked Buza Cruz.

"Are we talking dollars here?"

"We could be, I suppose. But I was thinking more in terms of . . . favours." Again aware of the value of her body, she knew plenty of ways of getting money. But the director of *The Trojan Horse* had the power to provide her with something much more valuable. She went on, "You scratch my back . . ."

Though von Klappentrappen had become pretty fluent in the language of his adopted country, there were still some idioms with which he was unfamiliar. "I have no desire to scratch your back," he protested.

"Put it this way, Gottie," said Buza, feeling increasingly confident of the power she had over him. "I'll tell you what you want to know . . . if you give me a better part in *The Trojan Horse*."

The director nodded. He was used to this kind of negotiation. And he was used to making generous offers that he had no intention of fulfilling. "Well," he said slowly, "there might be some way I could help you out there. The fact is, my new Helen of Troy . . ."

"Honoria Lyminster."

He nodded. "She's only been on the production for a few days, but I wonder whether she's going to be on it much longer . . ."

"Oh?"

"The fact is that I cast her on the say-so of Hank Urchief . . ."

"Ah."

". . . and I just wonder whether he's going to be as keen on having her around as he was when he first made the suggestion."

Buza Cruz nodded. Everyone working on *The Trojan Horse* had read Heddan Schoulders' column about Twinks's humiliation of the four major players at Toni Frangipani's party. She felt sure that von Klappentrappen was as keen to get the straight-talking troublemaker off the production as his male lead was.

Helen of Troy was a great part, the kind of part that would lift an anonymous starlet like Buza Cruz into the stratospheric world of stardom. There was a catch in her voice as she asked, "Are you offering me the job?"

"Well . . ." he hedged carefully. "Let's say there's likely to be a Helen of Troy-shaped hole in the cast of *The Trojan Horse* pretty damned soon, and I reckon you're pretty enough to play the most beautiful woman in the world."

The combination of flattery and carrot-dangling had the desired effect. But Buza Cruz still wanted to cover

152

all eventualities. "Are you offering me a contract to play Helen of Troy?"

He shrugged. "My lawyers deal with that kind of stuff. But they're pretty quick. First, they'll have to get on to Lefty Switzer to sort out the termination of Honoria Lyminster's contract, then I think damn soon after that there could be something for you to sign."

Buza Cruz flushed with excitement, showing once again that her acting range extended way beyond being turned to stone. "That's great," she murmured.

"So," said Gottfried von Klappentrappen casually, "the young man at Mimsy La Pim's party . . ."

"Yes."

"Can you give me a name?"

"No." The director looked disappointed, but the starlet assured him, "I'd recognise him if I saw him again."

This was not the kind of detailed information von Klappentrappen had been hoping for. The very distant possibility that Buza Cruz might take over the role of Helen of Troy was now firmly crushed. "Isn't there anything else you can tell me about him?"

"He was tall, blond, very good-looking."

The director had no wish to hear that. "Anything else?" he asked brusquely.

"Yes," said Buza Cruz. "He spoke with an English accent."

GRIM FOR VICTIM — WHICH CRIM SNATCHED LA PIM?

153

Big news today is that there's no news! Your friendly fact-flasher Heddan Schoulders has come up with a big zero, zilch on Mimsy La Pim. Like the dodo, that gorgeous girlie's vanished off the face of the eartheroonie. Who's taken the tottie? Is her kidnapping due to the company she keeps? Is there a guilty secret in her pasta? Has she been cosying up too close to the Cosa Nostra? Has there been a demand for a handsome ransom? Or is the hit hooked up with her Hollywood headlining? Is some dastardly devil about to rope her up to a railway line? Message to Mimsy: "We miss you!"

CHAPTER
EIGHTEEN

On the Trail of Mimsy La Pim

There was a vile calumny going around that Blotto was stupid, but sometimes he confounded all criticism by doing something very smart. And he reckoned that the next move he made in his search for Mimsy La Pim was very smart indeed.

His conversation with his sister had made him realise that he'd been duped by Lenny "The Skull" Orvieto, and that the Cosa Nostra was not the charitable institution he'd been led to believe. Twinks's words, endorsed by what Heddan Schoulders had written in her column, revived his opinion that there could well be an Italian connection to the fate of the kidnapped actress, so he needed to contact the Mafia once again.

Well, it had worked the last time . . .

He went to the same restaurant on Hollywood Boulevard, Giorgio's, and once again, as soon as the waiter offered him the menu, Blotto asked the same question. "Do you know how I can get in touch with the Mafia?"

The waiter was terrified all over again. He rushed once more to the telephone to conduct a panicky conversation, then returned to the table, asking if his customer would like a drink. Blotto again ordered a St Louis Steamhammer. When it was brought to the table, he took a sip and waited to be hit on the back of the neck by a lead-filled sock.

He was not disappointed. Giovanni and Giuseppe arrived right on cue and duly rendered him unconscious. When he came to, he was tied by his arms to the same chair in the same gilded room, facing Lenny "The Skull" Orvieto.

"We meet again, Mr Lyminster," said the Mafia boss, making no attempt to deny that he knew who his guest was. His whole manner was very different from the way he'd behaved on their previous encounter. This time he was in no mood for pretences about the Cosa Nostra being a charitable institution. In fact, he was seething with suppressed rage. The cranium reflected in the gilt-framed mirror behind him was slick with angry sweat. The snub-nosed automatic pistol on the desk was rather closer to him than it had been before.

"Toad in the hole, yes," said Blotto. "And I'm not prepared to listen to any more of your toffee. I now know about your relationship with Mimsy La Pim."

"Do you? And what would you say that relationship is?"

"A pretty fumacious one, if you want my checklist. Why would an innocent young woman like Mimsy La Pim associate with a stencher like you unless she was drugged or coerced into submitting to your murdy advances?"

Behind him Blotto heard a growl from either Giovanni or Giuseppe. "Shall I zap him again, boss?"

Lenny raised a hand in dissent. He needed more information before Blotto was returned to unconsciousness. "What's with the 'innocent young woman'? Do you *know* Mimsy La Pim?"

"Yes, I spoffing well do. She's as pure as the driven snow."

"You're wrong there. As pure as snow a few trucks have driven over, maybe."

"Are you looking for a bloody nose, Mr Orvieto?"

"Tied to that chair, Mr Lyminster, I don't think you're in a position to give anyone a bloody anything."

"Don't you believe it, Mr Orvieto," said Blotto defiantly. "My strength is as the strength of ten because my heart is pure."

The jaw in Orvieto's cavernous face dropped, revealing the teeth behind his thin lips and making their owner look more like a skull than ever. Clearly, whatever form of education he had undergone, either in Sicily or Los Angeles, had not, for some bizarre reason, encompassed the works of Alfred Lord Tennyson. After a moment, the Mafia boss recovered himself and asked, "Why do you think I might have anything to do with Mimsy La Pim's kidnapping? Why would I want to abduct my own broad?"

"Because maybe she stood up to you, told you what a lump of toadspawn you really are!"

"Shall I zap him now, boss?" came a growl from behind Blotto. He looked up at the mirror to see either Giovanni or Giuseppe handling his lead-filled sock eagerly. His associate, also keen for a bit of violence, had produced a wicked-looking butcher's knife from somewhere.

But again Lenny raised a hand to defer the immediate assault. "No, I'm interested in this fruitcake. You can have your fun in a little while, boys." The "boys" snarled with dissatisfaction at this delay while their boss turned again to their visitor. "So, Mr Lyminster, do you reckon you'll be able to find Mimsy La Pim?"

"Yes, by Wilberforce!"

"And how will you set about doing that? Do you have any leads as to where the poor little broad might be?"

Blotto was forced to admit that he hadn't. "But I'll get some!" he asserted defiantly.

"May I ask where from?"

"I'll get them from you, you four-faced filcher!"

Orvieto chuckled, but no humour glowed in his sunken eyes. "I don't think you're in any position to get anything from me, you scumdouche. You may not have noticed, but you're tied to a chair. We're armed and there are three of us."

Generations of breeding resonated in Blotto's voice as he declared, "Those are the kind of odds the Lyminsters have always favoured!"

Though anything theoretical would instantly befuddle his brain, in a practical emergency it worked with remarkable efficiency. He didn't have time to plan what he was to do next. The required actions were instinctively clear to him.

158

He stood up suddenly, lifting the chair with him. Then, his movements guided by what he could see in the mirror, he whirled round. The chair legs caught the first approaching Giovanni or Giuseppe in the shins and floored him, the lead-filled sock flying out of his hand.

Blotto turned to face the other Giovanni or Giuseppe, advancing with kitchen knife upraised. As the blade was brought ferociously down to stab him in the chest, Blotto executed another perfect whirl and the knife cut through the rope that bound his arms.

Released, Blotto threw a perfect upper cut at the jaw of the knife-wielding Giovanni or Giuseppe, then hurled the chair with all his strength at Lenny "The Skull" Orvieto. By the time the Mafia boss had regained his footing, he found himself looking down the snub-nosed barrel of his own automatic pistol, which his assailant had snatched up from the desk. (Blotto didn't really like the use of guns. He thought it was unsporting and would far rather have threatened Orvieto with his trusty cricket bat, but on this occasion he had to improvise with what was to hand.)

Giovanni and Giuseppe lurked against the walls, nursing their injuries and fearful of making any movement that might make Blotto pull the trigger.

"Maybe now you can see how I'm going to get my leads, you shifty sligger!" he said triumphantly.

"You kill me," Orvieto hissed, "and you'll have the whole Los Angeles Mafia after you! You won't last an hour!"

"That's a risk I'm prepared to take!" came the proud response. "Lyminsters have seen off worse stenchers

159

than that. We coffinated Anglo-Saxons during the Norman Conquest, infidels during the Crusades, and during the Wars of the Roses we saw off the . . ." He could never remember whether his ancestors had supported the White Rose of York or the Red Rose of Lancaster during that particular dust-up, so he finished rather lamely, ". . . the other side."

"The Mafia are more dangerous opponents than any of those."

"Huh, and huh again! Don't talk such toffee! Don't dare to start comparing ill-mannered Italian hoodlums to the Lyminsters' adversaries of yore." (Blotto still wasn't quite sure when, or what, "yore" was, but it sounded right in the context.) "Give me a lead on where to find Mimsy La Pim or you'll find you've got a real skull on top of your fumacious neck!"

The Mafia boss, believing the threat was real, instantly crumbled. "The Orvieto family had nothing to do with Mimsy La Pim's abduction. Like I said, I wouldn't want to kidnap my own tootsie. The people you want to talk to are the Barolo Brothers."

"Are they another bunch of Mafia slimers?"

Orvieto nodded. "They're really violent."

"Meaning that you aren't?"

"We do our best," the Mafia boss apologised, "but the Barolo Brothers . . . they take violence to a new level."

"Hoopee-doopee!" said Blotto. "There's nothing a Lyminster likes better than a spoffing challenge! And, incidentally," he continued, pushing the pistol barrel against Lenny's short nose, "if I find out that you've

160

been thimble-jiggling me and the Barolo Brothers have nothing to do with Mimsy's kidnapping . . . well, you'd better watch your back, Mr Orvieto. I know where you live."

Lenny Orvieto felt he had to pick Blotto up on a point of fact here. "Actually, technically you don't know where I live. You may recall that both times you've been brought here you've been unconscious. And when you left the last time you were blindfolded. So you don't know where I live."

"But I will soon, by Denzil! Because I'm going to leave this building with no blindfold on." He held out his hand. "Give me the key to that door."

Wordlessly, Orvieto reached into a drawer and handed over the key.

Blotto crossed to the door, the automatic pistol still trained on the mafia boss. Gesturing to the weapon, he said, "I'm going to keep this." He still wished he was talking about his cricket bat rather than a gun. "And I'm going to lock the door from the outside. It's up to you whether you smash it down or telephone some boddo to open it. But I promise you, try to come after me and, by Wilberforce, you'll regret it!"

"We don't need to come after you," said Orvieto in a last gesture of defiance. "You go after the Barolo Brothers and they'll deal with you and save us the trouble."

"Let's jump that hurdle when we come to it," said Blotto.

Then he left the room and locked the door from the outside. He waited for a moment, but heard no sounds of immediate pursuit.

Blotto walked through a lavishly decorated hall and out of a massive studded front door to find he was on the south side of Hollywood Boulevard within walking distance of the Hollywood Hotel.

He grinned and congratulated himself on a real buzzbanger of a morning's work.

CHAPTER
NINETEEN

The Barolo Brothers

Blotto's first instinct was to share the events of the morning with his sister. Though he was very pleased with what he'd achieved on his own, he knew that Twinks's superior intellect must be deployed in deciding what their next step should be.

To his surprise, he found no sign of Twinks in her suite and, on checking with reception, he was told that she'd been called to Humungous Studios for a day's filming as Helen of Troy on *The Trojan Horse*.

Blotto was rather put out by this news. He was unused to having a sister with demands on her time other than social commitments. The world of work was one in which he was a total stranger. He didn't know anyone in his circle whose life was dictated by the demands of something so menial as a job.

So he got the concierge to call a cab to take him to Humungous Studios.

Blotto's natural air of patrician authority got him past the gateman at the studio building and he was escorted on to the *Trojan Horse* set. There, Gottfried von Klappentrappen was once again bawling out Zelda

Finch, though Blotto didn't recognise her under her coronet of live snakes. The director was trying to get his wife to stay still for a shot, but though Zelda was the most professional of actresses, she could not overcome her phobia. As her husband grew angrier, his language, a mixture of English and German, grew riper.

The lighting technician running the book on the length of von Klappentrappen's latest marriage had stopped taking bets on it being over by the end of the month. Now the only odds he offered reckoned it wouldn't last the week.

Blotto was unconcerned about the main action in the studio, though. All he wanted to do was find Twinks. Passing someone who appeared to be dressed as a longhaired sheepdog, he asked after his sister's whereabouts and was surprised to hear a familiar voice saying, "How're you doing, my young feller-me-lad?"

He looked through the layers of hair and beard and recognised the eyes of J. Winthrop Stukes. "Toad in the hole!" he said. "What in the name of Denzil are you doing here?"

"I'm playing the part of Methuselah in the movie."

"Does that mean you're putting a candlesnuffer on the cricket?"

"Good Lord, no. Match next weekend, White Knights v. your chum Ponky Larreighffriebollaux's johnnies. Hope you'll be up for a knock . . .?"

"You'd have to strap me to a sleeping berth to keep me away!" responded Blotto, forgetting for the moment that he was going to devote his life to the Holy Gruel of rescuing Mimsy La Pim.

"Excellent, young feller-me-lad. One thing, though."

"Yes?"

"You're going to play for the White Knights, not the Peripherals."

"What? But the reason I actually pongled over the pond was to help out Ponky and —"

"And may I ask whose pitch you'll be playing on?" There was an edge of pique in Stukes's voice.

Blotto knew he was being suckered by the oldest ploy in the playground — the "it's my ball" argument — but J. Winthrop Stukes was his host as far as cricket was concerned. Reluctantly he agreed to turn out for the White Knights.

"Excellent news, young feller-me-lad. I'm sure we'll wipe the floor with them."

"Good ticket," said Blotto. Then he asked, "Haven't seen my sister pootling around, have you?"

"She was here a moment ago. She might have gone off to get her make-up repaired or something." The mass of hair shifted as J. Winthrop Stukes looked around. "Ah, there she is."

Twinks was walking towards them. In her latest Helen of Troy costume she looked more of a breathsapper than ever, but of course her brother never noticed things like that. "Hello, me old washboard," he greeted her. "Lots of ferrets to uncage on the Orvieto front."

"Splendissimo!" said Twinks. "Let's go back to the hotel and you can fill up my ears with facts there." She reached to pick her sequin-covered reticule.

"Erm, sorry, young lady," J. Winthrop Stukes interposed, "but you've been called on set today for a reason. When he's finished with the snake lady, Gottfried's about to shoot one of your scenes."

"Oh, stuff that for a taxidermist's dummy," Twinks responded casually. "I'm as bored as a frog who's off games with a strapped ankle. Tell Gottie I'm taking off the gauntlets. He'll have to find another Helen of Troy."

And so ended Twinks's career as a Hollywood actress. Still in costume — and in a high state of excitement — she hurried back with her brother to the Hollywood Hotel.

J. Winthrop Stukes didn't know the name of the starlet who approached him after the siblings' departure, but he had no objection to answering her query about the identity of the tall young blond man he'd just been talking to. The old actor didn't notice Buza Cruz go across during a break in shooting to whisper the name into the ear of Gottfried von Klappentrappen.

CHAPTER
TWENTY

Outside Help

"The Barolo Brothers," Twinks echoed. They were sitting in her suite as her brother brought her up to date with the events of his day. She had ditched her Helen of Troy garb and was now looking equally wonderful dressed in her own clothes.

"Do you know about them? The Barolo Brothers?" asked Blotto hopefully, always certain that his sister knew everything.

But in this case his confidence had been misplaced. Twinks shook her beautiful head. "But Orvieto said they were Mafia?"

"Tickey-Tockey." Blotto went on proudly, "And even though I may have been led through the shrubbery about the Cosa Nostra, I've always known that the Mafia are a criminal organisation." His sister, deep in thought, nodded distractedly. "And, Twinks me old pipe-cleaner, I've also always known that if you want to find out about criminals, you consult the local constabulary. Which out here is the L.A ... flipmadoodle."

"L.A.P.D." said Twinks.

"Yes, they're the boddoes. We should consult them."

"No, we shouldn't, Blotters. Out here probably the first thing the police would do if we made contact is let the Barolo Brothers know we're looking for them. And we'd lose our advantage of surprise."

"Do we have an advantage of surprise?"

"Only a very tiny one," said Twinks. "But it's about all we do have, so we shouldn't waste it."

"But how do we make contact with the Barolo Brothers? I suppose I could try my wheeze of going into Giorgio's on Hollywood Boulevard and asking about the Mafia, but I'm not sure the waiter Johnnie would be up for —"

"No, no," said Twinks. "I have a much better suggestion."

Blotto waited patiently. He knew that his sister's suggestions were always better than his own. "We've reached the point where we need outside help. And if you want information about anything — in Los Angeles or wherever — the most judderproof source is always acknowledged to be the finest university in the world."

She picked up the receiver and asked the hotel's telephonist to arrange for her to send a transatlantic cablegram. And she insisted it should go by Aristocratic Special Delivery.

The night porter at St Raphael's College Oxford was a romantic at heart. He thought, as a young man, that he had found true love when he met a young woman who introduced him to the delights of romantic novels. He grew addicted to such stories, as he grew addicted to the young woman who had introduced him to them.

168

He loved reading about young couples who met at the beginning of the narrative, were kept apart by various vicissitudes for most of the book's duration, then magically came back to each other at the end.

Unfortunately, the young woman who introduced him to such literature got rather too caught up in the vicissitudes that kept them apart (in her case, overlapping affairs with a surprising number of other young men) and omitted to come back to him at the end.

But whereas some young lovers would have been permanently embittered by such an experience, spending the rest of their lives railing against the perfidy of the opposite sex, the night porter at St Raphael's College Oxford took a more benign view. He had had his moment in the sun, but feared that if he ventured out again he might easily get burnt. Though still enjoying his romantic novels, in the pursuit of real love he thereafter regarded himself as a spectator rather than a participant. But nothing made him happier than the sight of another young couple feeling a mutual attraction and making the first steps into the thicket of vicissitudes that lay ahead.

His opportunities for witnessing such happy encounters, however, were limited. St Raphael's was a college of impeccable academic standards, but sadly it was an all-male institution. And the average age of its extraordinarily intelligent residents was at least seventy.

To further decrease the chances of love flourishing, since its foundation, St Raphael's had never admitted women on to the premises (or, to put it more accurately, the very few incidents of women being on the premises had always been hushed up).

So the night porter at St Raphael's College Oxford had some years before resigned himself to a diet of observing fictional rather than real-life romance. It should be pointed out that his role in the college was not exclusively that of night porter. He also fulfilled the same role during the day. But since, being only in his sixties, he was the most junior of the college porters, overnight duties were delegated to him and he slept in a comfortable room at the back of the porters' lodge.

The demands of the job were not onerous. Indeed, only once or twice a week were his slumbers interrupted by the ringing of the college doorbell and the need to let in one of the college fellows who had spent the evening in an excess of drinking (and who knew what other excesses).

So, when the bell rang that particular evening he rose from his bed and donned dressing gown and slippers in the expectation of greeting a familiar, if inebriated, face. He was surprised to be confronted by a young man in Post Office uniform delivering a cablegram, which had been sent by Aristocratic Special Delivery.

When he saw that the addressee was Professor Erasmus Holofernes and the sender's name was Honoria Lyminster, warmth glowed and grew to a flame in the night porter's heart. A cablegram of such urgency, he instantly presumed, could only be an expression of love. And though the professor, internationally renowned for his intellectual achievements, had a huge amount of mail delivered to the porters' lodge, never before had it included an urgent cablegram from a woman.

In spite of the hour, the night porter at St Raphael's College Oxford had no hesitation in ringing through immediately to the professor's rooms.

The professor's brain was acknowledged to be one of the hugest on the planet, a condition which, though bestowing many advantages, also brought with it some drawbacks. The chief of these was the dearth of equals on that same planet with whom he could conduct a meaningful conversation. Most of the people he met — even the high-powered fellows of St Raphael's — were, by his intellectual standards, rather dull.

Which was why he always welcomed any communication with Twinks. Though Holofernes would never admit that anyone's brain was superior to his own, hers came close. And though he was far too preoccupied with his studies to have any time for romantic feelings, even he would have to admit that her beauty provided an additional attraction to working with her.

She also always challenged him. If Twinks asked for information, it was a point of honour with Professor Erasmus Holofernes to see that he came up with the goods.

So, as soon as he had taken delivery of the cablegram, about whose contents the night porter at St Raphael's College Oxford had so inaccurately speculated, and it had been read, Holofernes leapt into action. With no thoughts of returning to bed until his mission was completed, with his shabby dressing gown untidily wrapped over his shabby pyjamas, he started to search for the information Twinks had requested.

Logic dictated that the room in which he worked must have had furniture in it somewhere, but none was visible under the chaos of documentation that covered every surface. The room looked like the aftermath of an explosion in a printing press. No outsider could have found anything in the mess of papers, but Professor Erasmus Holofernes had an immaculate homing instinct for what he needed.

And if Twinks wanted information about some Mafiosi in Los Angeles called the Barolo Brothers, that is what he would provide her with.

The professor's response, remarkably, reached the Hollywood Hotel within the day. When arranging her cablegram, Twinks had ensured that the reply was also sent by Aristocratic Special Delivery.

(Perhaps this is the moment to explain Aristocratic Special Delivery for the benefit of people born without silver spoons in their mouths. Blotto and Twinks were fortunate to live in an age when breeding still counted for something, and one of the perks was receiving all postal services much quicker than the plebs got them. Other rights assumed by birth included getting the best tables in restaurants, being allowed to run up large unpaid bills, patronising people of inferior breeding and, for the men in country houses, an endless supply of available chambermaids.)

But to return to the professor's cablegram. It read:

172

The Barolo Brothers are one of the most notorious Mafia gangs operating in California. They are noted for two things: their extreme violence and their almost total invisibility. Even other Mafiosi have no idea where their headquarters are. Nor how many there are in the gang or any of their names. All they know is that they brand the bodies of their victims with a distinctive "BB" insignia. However, my researches have unearthed clues to the Barolo Brothers' location and identity. Their cover is dressing as comic policemen employed in Hollywood movies, particularly the Krazy Kopz series produced by Humungous Studios. One of the Barolo Brothers is called Umberto. And if you need to put pressure on him, just say you know everything about the Japanese Theatre Stranglings. This is all I can find from the documentation I have to hand. If you require me to investigate further, that is, of course, something I am happy to do. Just let me know. As ever, I will be ready to drop all other demands on my time when I can help you, Twinks. All good wishes, Professor Erasmus Holofernes.

"Splendissimo!" cried Twinks. "Razzy's a Grade A Foundation Stone! He'll never let us down!"

CHAPTER
TWENTY-ONE

Kopz Kalamity!

Corky Froggett drove Blotto and Twinks down to Humungous Studios in the Lagonda. Having found his first few days in Los Angeles rather tedious (though he would never mention that fact to the young master), things had improved considerably for him since the young mistress had started to garner publicity for taking over the role of Helen of Troy in *The Trojan Horse*. In Hollywood there is always a gaggle of very attractive aspiring starlets who will do anything to achieve their breakthrough into the world of real stardom. For them contacts are everything, and to their minds being nice to the chauffeur of a rising star might ease that breakthrough. As a result, Corky Froggett had had a very pleasant few days.

When they reached the gates of the studios it was clear that news of Honoria Lyminster's defection from the cast of *The Trojan Horse* had not yet reached the security staff. Twinks asked the gateman where she would find the Krazy Kopz studio and was told, "They're out on one of the backlots, ma'am. Shooting *Krazy Kalamity*. Just follow the signs." Then the Lagonda was waved through with cheery smiles of welcome, while a few bulbs flashed as photographers tried to snatch some pics of the latest screen sensation.

Humungous Studios were laid out like a large village, with intersecting roads leading to the various lots and, as the gateman had said, signs indicating which movie was in production where. Twinks directed Corky Froggett away from *The Trojan Horse* set and the other studios, towards the backlot, where *Kopz Kalamity!* was being shot. A substantial fence stopped further progress, so he parked the Lagonda and was told to wait while Blotto and Twinks explored the area.

They walked through a variety of locations, which looked surprisingly solid, but were in fact three-sided façades built on wooden frames. From the main street of a Western town, complete with saloon and sheriff's office, their route took them past Swiss chalets backed by snow-covered mountains, a Russian winter palace, a French chateau and a sleepy Caribbean lagoon.

Then suddenly, rounding the corner of a medieval castle, they found themselves in the cross-fire of a custard-pie-throwing battle between opposing armies of men in blue police uniforms and helmets. All of the combatants had dead-white faces and their features had been exaggerated with black greasepaint. They knew they had found the set of *Krazy Kalamity!*

Blotto and Twinks ducked to avoid being splattered. They needn't have worried, though: the throwers were experts in the art. Their pies rose in neat parabolas before alighting inch-perfect on the faces of their selected opponents. As Blotto and Twinks emerged from the barrage and looked back they saw that one pie had just missed its target and landed on the shoulder of a blue uniform.

"Cut!" a voice snarled from the area behind the camera. Then, accusingly, "Who threw that?"

One small apologetic Krazy Kop stepped forward from the line.

"You're off the movie!" the voice snarled again. "You know we can't afford to clean the uniforms!"

The small policeman made no attempt at self-justification. He just slumped away, unbuttoning his jacket as he went, to face the miseries of Hollywood unemployment.

"Right, on to the next set-up — the truck scene!"

"We need to do a second take," an enormously fat Kop protested.

"We don't do second takes!"

"Well, this time you gotta."

"No!"

"But you can't use that last one." The fat Kop pointed towards Blotto and Twinks. "Those two boofers walked right through the middle of it."

"No worries," came the responding snarl. "Audience never notice stuff like that. Now get on with the truck set-up!"

Schooled in their routine, the Krazy Kopz reached for cloths to wipe the custard pie off their faces (carefully avoiding any residue dripping on their uniforms — they didn't want to share the fate of their small former associate). Then they hurried across to another part of the lot, some of them limping, and

176

started piling into the back of a dilapidated police truck.

Twinks noted with interest that one of the Krazy Kopz, tall and thin, didn't clean himself up after the battle. He didn't need to. No custard pie had landed on him. Having seen a lot of movies, Twinks recognised his role in the proceedings. Often in a slapstick routine there would be one person who, in a well-choreographed routine, would move from side to side or suddenly bend down, avoiding all the carefully timed missiles. Frequently at the climax of the scene the untouched individual would get hit by pies from all sides. It was of interest to Twinks that on this occasion that pay-off hadn't happened.

While the cameras were being moved to the new set-up, Twinks approached the director. "Pardon my poke-in," she said, "but I wondered if you could —"

"Can it!" snarled the director. "We've got three more movies to make today."

"Well, maybe when you have a break, we could —?"

"Break? What's with this break? We don't do breaks. We work on." He raised a megaphone to his lips and bellowed, demonstrating that he could do more than just snarl, "Are we ready with the truck set-up?"

"Nearly."

"Nearly's not good enough. We don't shout 'Action' within the minute, you lose your job!"

Realising she wasn't going to get through to the director, Twinks shrugged at Blotto and led him across to a couple of chairs from which they could see everything happening on the lot. "Keep the peepers peeled, Blotters," she said. "We need a clue."

"A clue," he echoed and lines of confusion appeared on his aristocratic brow. "Clue to what?"

"The whereabouts of Mimsy La Pim."

"Toad in the hole, yes." He felt rather guilty about forgetting his knightly quest, his Holy Gruel, and looked intently around the set. But he couldn't observe anything that might be classified as a clue.

As usual, though, he felt pretty confident that Twinks could.

The set-up for the truck scene had now been completed. The back of the open vehicle was full of Krazy Kopz with truncheons ready to wave. In the driver's seat sat a tall policeman awaiting his cue. A member of the stage crew had turned the crank handle to start up the vehicle and its engine was roaring away. The truck was on a short stretch of road that led to, and then curved away from, an artificial lake which wasn't very wide, but at the end of it a *trompe-l'oeil* was painted on a wall to make it look more extensive. On a park bench facing the lake, just where the road curved, sat a young couple canoodling.

"Action!" the director snarled.

At the command the driver engaged gear and the loaded truck leapt forward. It trundled along at speed, seemed about to follow the curve of the road, but instead flew across the kerb to smash into the back of the park bench. The seat itself stood firm, but the canoodling couple were ejected straight into the lake.

178

At the same time, some mechanism was released so that the back of the truck flipped up, catapulting its load of truncheon-waving Kops over the driver's cab and into the lake.

At the moment they splashed in, the doors fell off both sides of the truck and a plume of smoke rose up from its crushed frontage.

"Cut!" yelled the director. "Move on to the painting scene!"

Blotto and Twinks watched the Krazy Kopz pick themselves out of the lake and hobble across to the next set-up. Some looked as if they'd been painfully injured by their flight from the back of the truck, but there were no murmurs of dissent. They all knew how easy it was to lose your job in Hollywood.

Blotto and Twinks did hear one of the Kops ask the director, "Don't we get time to dry off our uniforms?"

"No," came the snarled reply. "On the movie it won't show whether they're wet or dry! Get to the painting set-up!"

This scene used one of the backlot's permanent structures, the façade of an apartment block, against which a framework of wooden scaffolding had been erected. On boards at the various levels of the structure had clambered the company of various-sized Krazy Kopz. Some carried paintbrushes, others buckets of whitewash. At the director's shout of "Action!" they started to mime painting the building. (Twinks reckoned they were only miming so that, like their uniforms, the frontage wouldn't have to be cleaned afterwards.)

While the policemen mimed painting above, down at street level some more action was taking place. An attractive young woman walked along the sidewalk past the apartment block with a huge, but apparently docile, mastiff on a lead. At the end of the scaffolding she stopped, looked at the dress shop next door and mimed elaborately that she wanted to enter and inspect their stock. Tying the mastiff's lead to the nearest wooden scaffolding upright, she disappeared into the shop.

At this point, a tall Krazy Kop came strolling along the sidewalk from the same direction as the young woman. He moved with nonchalance, twirled his truncheon and, though he was in a silent film, whistled. As he passed the mastiff, the dog, who had clearly undergone training and rehearsal, bared its teeth at him. The Kop looked down at the animal and, keeping a safe distance away, stuck his tongue out. The dog growled (though again the viewers in the picture palaces would only see rather than hear its rage).

The policeman was beginning to enjoy the game. He crouched down and, sticking his fingers in his ears, flapped his hands to further antagonise his quarry. The mastiff leapt forward, lead straining against the wooden post to which it was attached.

Then the Kop got bored. He stood up and, again twirling his truncheon and whistling, strolled past the dress shop and out of shot.

As a result, so far as the movie-goer was concerned, the policeman didn't know what the results of his actions were. The set must have been carefully prepared for what happened when the mastiff's drag on its lead pulled the restraining post away from its footing.

The entire scaffolding structure came down, scattering planks and struts, paint pots and Krazy Kopz in every direction.

Though the director didn't "do breaks", the next scenes he had to shoot — blowing up a couple of cars — didn't involve any human beings. Even in Krazy Kopz productions there were some safety limits and, to the director's patent disappointment, his superiors had decreed that the bodies thrown sky-high by the explosions would have to be dummies. So Blotto and Twinks finally got an opportunity to pursue their investigation.

"Well, I didn't see any spoffing clues," said Blotto.

"I did," said Twinks, predictably enough.

While the director and his cameramen had left the immediate area, the Krazy Kopz had picked themselves up and stumbled in through the door of an Episcopal cathedral façade. The smells of liniment and embrocation emanating from the building suggested that it was a kind of field hospital to treat the numerous bruises and fractures suffered in the manufacture of Krazy Kopz slapstick.

Blotto was about to enter, but Twinks stopped him. "No, no, Blotters. Our quarry isn't in there."

"What? By Wilberforce, do you mean you know who he is?"

"Oh yes."

"But how, in the name of strawberries?"

"Did you notice, Blotto me old headache powder, that only one of the Krazy Kopz didn't get hurt in any of the scenes we've just witnessed? He wasn't touched by a custard pie, he was the driver of the truck that chucked everyone else into the lake, and he was one who made fun of the dog and moved on. Didn't you notice that?"

"No," said Blotto, honest as ever.

"Well, it's true. Which of course means that he has some privileged position here in the Krazy Kopz set-up. Razzy told us that this is where the Barolo Brothers operate, so I'd put my last shred of laddered silk stocking on the fact that the one who escaped all the painful stuff is connected to the Barolo Brothers. What's more," continued Twinks, leading her brother towards a swish first class railway carriage stranded rather absurdly on a few yards of track, "I saw him go in here."

The light let in by her opening the door made the man inside the carriage look up. Dark-haired and very thin, he was resting on a *chaise-longue*. A bottle of Bourbon stood on the table beside him and the glass on the way to his lips was frozen in midair.

"It's creamy éclair to meet you," said Twinks, "Umberto."

CHAPTER
TWENTY-TWO

Confrontation in a Carriage

The man reached to the pocket of his Krazy Kopz uniform for a gun, but was stopped by Twinks saying, "You'd be a total soft-top to do that, Umberto . . . seeing what I've got in my hand."

The Mafioso and Blotto looked with equal surprise at the small snub mother-of-pearl-handled Derringer that Twinks had whipped out of her sequined reticule. In fact, Blotto's surprise was probably the greater. In most of their escapades he and his sister had not resorted to firearms. Neither felt that their use was quite "playing the game". It was fair enough to use a firearm knocked out of an adversary's grasp, but for more general combat Blotto preferred to rely on his trusty cricket bat. He regretted that he didn't have it with him at that moment. He must remember to pick the thing up from the hotel before embarking on the next stage of their adventure.

And he must remember to ask Twinks why she had resorted to having a Derringer at the ready, though now probably wasn't the moment.

Umberto didn't go any further in producing his own gun, but he chuckled lazily and said, "You think I'm afraid of that little peashooter."

"It may look like a peashooter, but it can still kill you as sure as a bedtime yawn. Don't forget, Umberto, it was one of these little bellbuzzers that did for your President Lincoln."

The smile stayed on the Mafioso's face. "Yeah, babe, but you only got two barrels. You shoot that thing at me twice, you miss me twice, you have to reload. Giving me time to draw out my revolver and pump six helpings of lead into your gut."

"You wouldn't do that, you stencher!" asserted Blotto gallantly. "Because I would stand between my sister and the bullets."

Umberto took this on board. "OK, bud. You stand in front of her, I pump three into your gut. You fall down, I pump the other three into hers. Equal rights for men and women, huh?"

Blotto had to admit that this sounded reasonable, but his train of thought was interrupted by Twinks saying, "One little thingette you have failed to take account of in your thought-throwing, Umberto, is that if I shoot this little peashooter at you, I won't miss. And I certainly won't miss twice."

Something in the way she spoke gave him pause. He quailed, as he might have done were he facing the Dowager Duchess. And when Twinks ordered Blotto to take his revolver, Umberto did not resist.

"I'd better put this slug-shifter somewhere safe," said Blotto, looking around the carriage.

"You don't put it somewhere safe!" said Twinks, coming as near to exasperation as she ever did with her brother. "You cock it and point it at this lump of toadspawn's head . . ."

"Tickey-Tockey." Her brother did as instructed.

". . . so that we can show him we mean business."

"Meaning," said Umberto, whose confidence was clearly returning, "that there are now two people to shoot me if I don't co-operate?"

"You're bong on the nose there," said Twinks. "Give that pony a rosette."

"OK." The Mafioso was grinning again now. "But there's one — if I may use your word, 'thingette' — which means I ain't trembling in my boots too much at the prospect of being filled fuller of holes than a colander by you, and that is that I don't think either of you would actually pull the trigger."

"If you think that," said Twinks in a tone of icy defiance, "then you've plumped for the wrong plum."

"Oh yeah?" He looked coolly at Twinks. "You wouldn't shoot me."

"I'd think no more of it than I would of crushing a cockroach under my ballet pump."

Again he believed her, so he turned the beam of his argument on to what he reckoned to be the weaker partner. "How about you, buddy boy? You ever shot anyone in cold blood?"

"Well, I . . . er . . . um . . ." Blotto was torn between his desire to support Twinks and his instinct for honesty. "Well, not as such."

Umberto pressed forward his advantage. "Have you ever actually fired a gun?"

"Oh yes, by Denzil. Given an air gun for my second birthday. Bagged twenty rabbits and a hare before I was three. Oh, and a nurserymaid . . . but it was her fault, she stepped in front of the hare."

"And shooting in cold blood?" Umberto persisted.

The conflict within Blotto was expressed in a deep blush as he admitted, "No, I wouldn't shoot anything in cold blood . . . well, except for a partridge, obviously . . . or a pheasant . . . or a stag, come to that. But people, no . . . Not cricket. A boddo has to dig a trench somewhere, you know."

"Blotto," Twinks hissed, "you're not helping my argument."

"No, he isn't, is he?" Umberto rose nonchalantly from the table and walked towards them. "So I reckon I'm pretty safe. Little Lord Fauntleroy here has admitted he won't shoot me and you, sugarbabe, you ain't going to shoot me till you got some information. So I reckon there's nothing to stop me from stepping out that door, rousing up the rest of the Barolo Brothers and clearing the United States of America of two more undesirable immigrants."

Blotto made no move to stop him, but as the crook walked past Twinks, she said softly, "It just so happens, Umberto me old tea-strainer, that I know everything about the Japanese Theatre Stranglings."

She hadn't fired a bullet from her Derringer, but nothing short of that could have stopped him so suddenly in his tracks. His confidence crumbled. He seemed physically to diminish in stature before their eyes. In a cracked voice, he asked, "You're not about to tell the other Barolo Brothers about that, are you?"

"That rather depends," replied Twinks evenly, "on whether you give me the information I require or not."

Within two minutes Umberto had told them not only where Mimsy La Pim was being held, but also the fate that was being prepared for her.

"Larksissimo!" cried Twinks, as Corky Froggett drove them back to the Hollywood Hotel. "Razzy really is a Grade A foundation stone! How he gets that kind of detailed information from his room in St Raphael's I will never know."

"So," asked Blotto, "what happened in the Japanese Theatre Stranglings? And how was that thimble-jiggler Umberto involved in them?"

"I haven't a batsqueak of an idea," his sister replied airily, "but the fact that Umberto *thought* I knew turned the tumblers like a good 'un, so everything else is lah-di-dah and pom-pi-pom."

Blotto could not but agree. Both were in jubilant mood. At last their investigation was getting somewhere. Twinks, who had been becoming jolly bored with being Hollywood's latest screen sensation, now had a challenge worthy of her planet-sized brain. And, though he didn't mention it to his sister, Blotto was secretly rather excited about the imminent prospect of seeing Mimsy La Pim again.

But the next stage, Twinks was all too aware, wouldn't be easy. Though the information they'd got from Umberto represented a huge step forward, they would still have to defeat the full power of the Barolo Brothers to rescue the kidnapped star.

Her brother, though, didn't have any such qualms. "Corky," he called out, "don't take us back to the hotel. We're going to the Barolo Brothers' HQ!"

"No, we're not," said Twinks calmly. "Corky, drive to the Hollywood Hotel!"

The chauffeur brought the Lagonda to a sedate halt and waited. He had experienced many such differences of opinion between the siblings over the years. He knew that Twinks's opinion would always eventually hold sway, but he also knew that they had to go through the ritual of an argument before that happy resolution was reached.

"Well, you may have a pointette, Twinks me old sherry trifle," Blotto finally conceded, and Corky Froggett put the car back into gear.

By the time the Lagonda drew up outside the Hollywood Hotel, having firmly rejected Blotto's suggestions, they — or rather Twinks — had decided their immediate plan of action. She wanted to evaluate what their next step should be, and to do that she needed to spend a couple of hours alone in her suite, basically just thinking. Blotto, aware of his limitations, knew that this was an area where he could contribute little, and so he was happy to accept his sister's recommendation that he should do a little reconnaissance of the location where the next stage of the drama would be played out. So, with only a minor delay while he fetched his cricket bat from his suite, Blotto returned to the Lagonda and gave Corky directions to their destination.

In both siblings the jubilant mood continued. Whether it would have done had they known about the other dangers that threatened them is not so certain.

CHAPTER
TWENTY-THREE

Exchange of Contracts

The fact was that a lot of people were rather angry with Blotto and Twinks. The cause of the anger in each case was the same: bruised ego. And that was the one part of the Hollywood anatomy that nobody could bruise without anticipating a comeback.

The Mafia ego was equally sensitive.

And there was no denying that Lenny "The Skull" Orvieto's ego had received a severe battering when he was locked in his own office by some limey swell. What was more, his ego-battering had been witnessed by two of his own men, Giovanni and Giuseppe. That kind of thing didn't sit well with the self-image — not to mention reputation — of Lenny "The Skull" Orvieto.

True, he'd said he wouldn't need to come after Blotto because the Barolo Brothers would get him. Which might be true. But the idea of such a resolution stuck in his craw. He, Lenny, was the one who'd been made to look a dumbo. He, Lenny, should be the one to revenge the insult.

He brooded on the matter for some time after he'd had to phone one of his security team to let him out of his office — another indignity, and he wasn't sure the man had believed the story about him having mislaid his key. (Of course, he could have got out by getting Giovanni and Giuseppe to break the door down, but the place had recently been professionally decorated and Orvieto liked things to look good. He was as dandyish about his environment as he was about his clothes.)

It took only a couple of hours' brooding before Lenny decided he had to take action. Blotto had not only shamed him personally, he had brought dishonour on the whole Orvieto family. If news of what had happened got around the other Mafia gangs — particularly the Barolo Brothers — his family would become objects of ridicule. Something had to be done. Orvieto summoned Giovanni and Giuseppe.

"The guy who was just here . . ." he began.

"The guy who locked us in?" suggested Giovanni or Giuseppe.

Their boss winced. There was no need to remind him. But he just nodded, then drew a finger across his throat.

Giovanni and Giuseppe understood. They knew what was required of them. A contract had just been taken out on Blotto's life.

They would have left straight away to get on with their mission, had not a visitor been announced by their boss's very pretty (but strictly untouchable) secretary. It was Toni Frangipani.

Giovanni and Giuseppe watched as the two men greeted each other with huge hugs. Their association went back a long way. Indeed, before Frangipani's career had started, Orvieto had been thinking of getting a foothold in the movie business before the other Mafia gangs muscled in. And he'd decided the best approach would be to develop a Hollywood star who owed all his success to the Orvieto family.

Lenny relied on teenage girl cousins back in the old country to pick the right candidate, trusting that they would know what kind of man turned them on. And they selected a Sicilian itinerant grape-treader called Baldassare Zappacosta, whose attraction to the opposite sex had been validated by at least a dozen unwanted pregnancies.

The young man was shipped over to the States and targeted on Hollywood stardom by all the means the Orvieto family had at their command. The name Baldassare Zappacosta was very quickly replaced by the more euphonious Toni Frangipani. In New York he was taught basic manners and kitted out with an extensive wardrobe. In case he might be feeling amorous, he was introduced to a lot of "nice young ladies" who were "nice" to him as if their lives depended on it (as indeed they did).

When Lenny "The Skull" Orvieto thought the boy was ready, Toni Frangipani was transported to Hollywood. There he attracted the interest of some major producers. (Amazing how easily some people's interest can be attracted when their families are being threatened.) And he also began to do very well at auditions. (Again, amazing how easy it is to get parts when all the other candidates are found dead in burnt-out cars.)

In short, within a few months, Toni Frangipani was one of the biggest stars in the movies. The one possible threat to his acting career — the fact that he had a very squeaky voice and hardly spoke English — couldn't have mattered less in the silent era.

He never forgot — indeed, he would have been very unwise to forget — how much he owed every step of his career to Lenny "The Skull" Orvieto.

And, because Lenny was a generous guy, the relationship between them was a two-way street. If Toni Frangipani wanted something organised, Lenny was usually happy to organise it for him.

That afternoon Toni Frangipani wanted something organised. If Twinks's snub had only been witnessed by those present, it would soon have been forgotten. But because Heddan Schoulders had written it up in her column — and kept writing little reminders of the incident in subsequent columns — Hollywood showed no signs of forgetting. And each mention thumped yet another bruise on to his already-bruised ego.

"So," Lenny "The Skull" Orvieto asked him that afternoon, "what needs doing?"

"I needa someone taken outa."

Giovanni and Giuseppe looked alert. He was talking their language.

"No problem," said Orvieto. "The boys'll take care of it. So who is he?"

"No 'he'. Issa 'she'."

"Name?"

"Honoria Lyminster."

Lenny "The Skull" Orvieto looked at his two hoods and passed the finger across his throat.

A contract had just been taken out on Twinks's life.

$\star \quad \star \quad \star$

The Atchison, Topeka and Santa Fe Railroad's La Grande Station was a familiar destination for tourists visiting Los Angeles (though neither Blotto nor Twinks had ever heard of it). Under its Moorish dome, as well as the railroad tracks and the platforms, there was a rabbit warren of offices. Most of these, obviously, were connected to the business of transportation, and the average person passing a door whose brass plate read "Terminal Services" would have assumed it was part of the same network. They would, however, have been wrong.

It was quiet that afternoon in the office behind the door. The two clerks who manned the office sat in their shirtsleeves reading the racing papers. The windows were open and the fan, which turned turgidly from its ceiling mounting, didn't do enough to make the thick air move.

They were used to days like this. There wasn't really a pattern to the demand in their line of business. Days, weeks would go past without even an enquiry. Then suddenly there could be a flurry of half a dozen jobs within a week. The two clerks didn't worry. They knew that when the work did come in it paid well. Their continuing employment was not under threat.

And of course, their job was only the fixing. They were the initial point of contact. All transactions were completely anonymous. Clients tended to have accounts. When they rang they gave their account number, which acted as a password. They then gave the job specifications. The clerk who answered the phone would quote a price which, though enormous, was never questioned. That call would end and the clerk, using another password, would ring the relevant number. Neither of the clerks had ever met the men who fulfilled their clients' requirements.

In the middle of that stifling afternoon, the telephone rang. One of the clerks picked up the receiver. "Good afternoon. Terminal Services."

The caller gave his account number.

"Thank you. One moment, sir." The clerk checked through a card index on his desk to find the client's details. "Very good, sir. And could I ask you for the name of the person for whom you wish to employ Terminal Services?"

The name was given. The clerk, an avid reader of the Hollywood gossip columns, recognised it immediately but, in accordance with his training, betrayed no emotion as he repeated the name to check he'd got it right.

"Yup," said the voice from the other end of the line.

"And do you wish the job to be carried out as soon as possible?"

"Yup," the voice confirmed.

"Let me just get you a price for that . . ." The clerk knew full well the amount that was going to be demanded but, again as instructed during his training, he made the sounds of checking through some paperwork. He then quoted an eye-wateringly large figure. "Will that be in order, sir?"

"Yup."

"Very good, sir. The job will be done and the fee added to your usual monthly account. Will that be in order, sir?"

"Yup."

"And is there anything else we can help you with this afternoon?"

"Nope."

"Well, thank you very much, sir, for using Terminal Services. Satisfaction, as always, guaranteed."

The call was ended. Back on his ranch, which covered large chunks of Texas, Wilbur T. Cottonpick, dressed in another screamingly loud suit, sat back in his chair with some satisfaction. Though only an investor in the movie business, his ego was at least as sensitive as a film star's. He had been held up to ridicule in Heddan Schoulders' column. No one held Wilbur T. Cottonpick up to ridicule and survived.

And another contract had just been taken out on Twinks's life.

Hardly had that call ended than the telephone again rang in the airless office. The clerk who'd just been busy gestured to his colleague to take this one.

"Good afternoon. Terminal Services."

The account number was given and an almost identical conversation ensued.

The clerk concluded it, "Well, thank you very much, sir, for using Terminal Services. Satisfaction, as always, guaranteed."

Beside one of the pools at his Hollywood mansion, Hank Urchief lay back on his lounger, feeling sure he'd made the right decision. Not only would the assault on his ego be revenged, but he also saw a way of gaining sympathy — and publicity — by a very ostentatious display of grief at his victim's demise. "So much talent

. . . such a great future . . . tragic to see a young life cut off so early . . .”

And another contract had just been taken out on Twinks's life.

The two clerks in the Terminal Services offices looked at each other in disbelief as the phone rang for the third time that afternoon. After a few slack weeks, business was really hotting up.

The clerk who'd taken Hank Urchief's call gestured that it was his colleague's turn.

“Good afternoon. Terminal Services.”

The routine was sedately repeated, but this one was different. The client gave two names rather than one. When the call ended, the clerks looked at each other in delighted disbelief. Four jobs within an hour had to be some kind of record. They felt very pleased with themselves.

Gottfried von Klappentrappen felt pretty pleased with himself too. Nobody gave him the brush-off and got away with it, and they certainly didn't compound that felony by walking out of one of his movies.

He was also pleased to be getting rid of the young man who had made him look a fool by conducting a dalliance with his wife Zelda Finch. Soon to be ex-wife, Gottfried von Klappentrappen thought with some satisfaction.

Umberto found himself in a dilemma. He had been totally outmanoeuvred by Twinks, and that dumb brother of hers had witnessed his humiliation. For a man of his proud Sicilian ancestry, revenge was essential.

But his normal method of revenge was not open to him. Usually, when someone slighted him, he did what any other of the Barolo Brothers would have done and turned to the family for support. The massed power of the gang could track down and obliterate Blotto and Twinks within minutes.

But in this instance he couldn't let his relations know about his dishonour. To do that would inevitably bring up his involvement in the Japanese Theatre Stranglings, an incident in his life over which a veil had been conveniently drawn. If the rest of the Barolo family found out that he had betrayed them on that occasion, then the contract would be taken out on him rather than Blotto and Twinks.

It was a ticklish situation. But the more he thought about it, the more Umberto realised that he couldn't allow the English girl to walk around Hollywood knowing about the Japanese Theatre Stranglings, whose details she could unload to any willing listener whenever she chose to. Her brother must also know about his act of disloyalty to the Barolo Brothers.

So both of them had to be eliminated as soon as possible. And since he couldn't turn to his usual recourse of the family, he would have to do the job himself.

Mentally, he took out personal contracts on both the siblings.

The score at the end of the day was that Blotto had three contracts out on his life, but Twinks was way ahead with five.

CHAPTER
TWENTY-FOUR

The Plot Thickens – Again!

Blotto was pleased with the reconnaissance trip he'd taken with Corky Froggett. Though Umberto had revealed where Mimsy La Pim was being held, he'd made a very strong indication that rescuing her from there was not a sensible option.

Blotto's instinctive reaction when he heard that advice was to regard it as a challenge. All right, so Mimsy was incarcerated in the Barolo Brothers' headquarters in the Hollywood Hills, surrounded by dozens of armed guards. Well, those were the kind of odds he liked. Nothing appealed to him more than the idea of storming the citadel single-handed with no weapon other than his trusty cricket bat.

But wiser counsel from Twinks had curbed that instinct. As Umberto had admitted, the time when the Barolo Brothers would be most vulnerable would be the following morning, as they moved Mimsy La Pim from her incarceration to the place where they intended her to spend her final minutes. That was when any rescue attempt should be made.

Because Umberto had revealed the location where the stenchers planned to liquidate the poor innocent girl, that was where Blotto and Corky had gone to reconnoitre. And Blotto was very excited by what he saw. It was the ideal place for cricket-bat-waving heroics.

He could hardly wait for the next morning. Not only would he finally remeet Mimsy La Pim, he would also save her life. And he knew that doing that kind of thing could help to put a boddo in a girl's good books.

So, with a merry "Chinny-up!" to Corky Froggett as the Lagonda deposited him at the entrance to the Hollywood Hotel, Blotto rushed up the stairs, longing to share with Twinks the discoveries of the afternoon.

He burst into her suite to find it empty.

A sheet of paper was pinned to the dressing table by a vicious-looking knife.

On it were scrawled the words: "WE'VE GOT HONORIA LYMINSTER. YOU WILL BE CONTACTED ABOUT THE RANSOM ARRANGE-MENTS."

Twinks had been kidnapped!

Suddenly Blotto was in a quest for two Holy Gruels.

CHAPTER
TWENTY-FIVE

Corky Fills the Role

Blotto was at a loss. The similarity between the two notes made it clear, even to him, that Twinks had probably been kidnapped by the same lumps of toadspawn who'd taken Mimsy La Pim. In other words, the Barolo Brothers.

His first instinct had been to rush straight round to their headquarters, armed with his cricket bat, and rescue both victims. But he remembered how strongly Twinks had condemned this plan of action when there had been only one person incarcerated. Would she be of the same opinion now that there were two?

If only Twinks were there for him to ask . . .

"Broken biscuits!" he said out loud right there in her suite, which was a measure of how distraught he was.

He needed a sounding board. Though he was very good at *doing* action, he was a bit of an empty revolver when it came to *planning* action. He scoured his brain for names of people with whom he could discuss the problem. Ponky Larreighffriebollaux . . .? Though one of his favourite muffin-toasters and an absolute foundation stone on the cricket field — there was no one Blotto would rather have at the other end when building up a fourth wicket stand — Ponky didn't have a planning brain. J. Winthrop Stukes . . .? He seemed an amiable cove, certainly knew his cricket and played a straight bat. On the other hand, the more time Blotto spent in Hollywood, the less able he felt to trust anyone involved in the movie business.

No, it was really Twinks he needed to consult with.

He wondered for a moment whether it was because he was away from home that the problem seemed so acute. But no, back at Tawcester Towers without Twinks he'd still be caught like a lobster in a mangle.

On the other hand, back at home, he could always commune with Mephistopheles. But though he got lots of moral support from that source, the hunter was never that useful when it came to giving practical advice.

And the only other person at Tawcester Towers he communed with was . . . Suddenly it came to him. Corky Froggett!

He found the chauffeur resolutely polishing the Lagonda in the parking garage underneath the hotel. The blue bodywork looked perfect, but it was a point of honour with Corky to remove every fleck of dust within minutes of its landing on the surface. He even kept a weather eye, with his chamois leather at the ready, to trap as many flecks as he could before they achieved landfall.

"Good afternoon, milord," he said, standing instinctively to attention at the young master's approach. He only just stopped himself from saluting.

202

Corky Froggett's time in the military had left a mark on every aspect of his life. Particularly in revealing to him where his true talent lay, which was in the business of killing people.

"Corky old chum . . ." said Blotto, using language that would have appalled the Dowager Duchess, who had no truck with the alien concept of treating the servant classes as if they were part of the same species. "I'm in a bit of a gluepot."

"Sorry to hear that, milord."

The roof of the Lagonda was still down from its recent excursion. Blotto got in the driver's seat and draped himself over the leather upholstery. He patted the seat beside him. "You get in, Corky."

"I think it would be more appropriate were I to stand, milord."

"And if I were to order you to get in and sit down . . .?"

"Then I would obviously do as instructed, milord."

"Well, I am."

"You are what, milord?"

"I am ordering you to get in and sit down."

"Very good, milord." Corky Froggett got in and sat down. But he didn't look very relaxed. He had the rare ability to sit as if he were still standing at attention.

There was a silence. Whereas other people might have asked Blotto the nature of the gluepot in which he found himself, the chauffeur did not feel it was his place to initiate conversation.

Finally, Blotto spoke. "Fact is, not to fiddle around the furniture, Corky, Twinks has been kidnapped."

"How very unfortunate for the young mistress." Then Corky saw a possible way of realising his lifetime's ambition. "If it were of use, milord, for me to beard the kidnappers in their lair, to lay down my life in an unsuccessful attempt to rescue your sister, you have only to say the word."

"Well, that's very sporting of you, Corky, but actually I was thinking a *successful* attempt to rescue the old bloater might fit the pigeonhole rather better."

"Oh." The chauffeur could not completely keep the disappointment from his voice. Since he had first started working as a boot boy at Tawcester Towers, he had aspired to the apotheosis of laying down his life for a member of the Lyminster family. But it seemed that would have to wait for another occasion. He quickly readjusted his expectations and asked, "Do you know who has kidnapped the young mistress, milord?"

"It's a guinea to a groat that this is the work of a bunch of stenchers called the Barolo Brothers."

"Ah." The name meant nothing to Corky. He knew little of the criminal underworld of Los Angeles. "And do you know where these devilish monsters have taken the young lady?"

"I can't actually guarantee I've winged the right partridge, but I'm pretty sure the Barolo Brothers are holding her in their HQ."

"And where's that?"

"It's a disused backlot. Hasn't been used for many years, but it's dressed up as a mountain hideout . . . you know, the kind of swamphole where the bad tomatoes who've been terrorising the local cattle ranchers hole up and divide their spoils? And where they take their kidnap victims, come to that."

"Like they did in *Chaps' Lonesome Stand?*"

Blotto looked at his chauffeur in amazement. "Have you seen that?" he asked.

"Certainly, milord. You try to keep me away from the Tawsford Picture Palace when there's a Chaps Chapple movie on."

"Toad in the hole, Corky, you're not telling me you're a Chaps Chapple enthusiast?"

"Certainly am, milord."

"Well, I'll be jugged like a hare! I've seen every one of his movies about a dozen times."

"Me too, milord. And, what's more, that makes me think of a way we might rescue the young mistress!"

"How's that, Corky? Come on, uncage the ferrets."

"Well, milord, you remember what Chaps Chapple does in *Chaps' Lonesome Stand . . .?*"

CHAPTER
TWENTY-SIX

Blotto's Lonesome Stand

The levels of secrecy employed by the Terminal Services operation were very tight. Information was shared on a need-to-know basis. The use of a complex system of codes meant that no member of the network knew the identity of any others.

This worked splendidly most of the time, as could be vouched for by the number of successful liquidations achieved by the company, but it did have one unconsidered drawback.

Because of the lack of direct contact between the fixers and the perpetrators, each new job was treated in isolation, with no sharing of information. As a result, in the rare event of two contracts being taken out on the same person, two hitmen would be allocated as if they were doing two separate jobs.

Which meant that, though only one Terminal Services hitman was delegated to kill Blotto, three had been given the job of killing Twinks.

And, of course, Giovanni and Giuseppe were on a mission to kill both of them.

Early the following morning, in separate anonymous Los Angeles apartments, four hitmen checked that their weapons of choice — automatic pistols — were in perfect working order.

Meanwhile, in Lenny "The Skull" Orvieto's headquarters, Giovanni and Giuseppe did the same.

Blotto's instinct, when talking to Corky Froggett in the Hollywood Hotel garage, had been to rush straight to the Barolo Brothers' hideout, but the chauffeur had deterred him. Filling the role of Twinks rather well, he had advised spending some time planning their assault before taking action. Grudgingly, Blotto had been forced to agree.

The idea occurred to both of them at the same time that it would be jolly useful, before they faced the real-life situation, to have another viewing of *Chaps' Lonesome Stand*. Surely, in Hollywood, centre of the movie world, arranging such a viewing shouldn't be too difficult.

Nor was it. Remembering that J. Winthrop Stukes had talked about having a private cinema, Blotto rang through to Britannia. The actor was delighted to hear from the new star of the White Knights cricket team, even more delighted to hear that Blotto wanted to use his private cinema, though considerably less delighted when he heard that it wasn't one of his own movies they wanted to watch.

The arrangement was, however, made. Blotto and Corky spent an enchanted evening watching Chaps Chapple once again surmounting all odds to rescue the beautiful innocent young girl from the hideout of the O'Connor gang. They were spellbound right to the

207

moment when Chaps touched the brim of his leather hat to the lady and rode off into the sunset.

J. Winthrop Stukes, who'd been the perfect host all evening, then asked if they'd like to watch one of his movies next. He was considerably less genial when they said they wouldn't.

"Absolutely the lark's larynx, that film, isn't it?" said Blotto as Corky eased the Lagonda back to the Hollywood Hotel.

"It certainly is, milord."

"I love the rolling of the barrels, sending the O'Connors flying, and all that rombooley, don't you?"

"Certainly do, milord."

"And that swinging down on the rope bit at the end — if that isn't the panda's panties, what is?"

"Nothing, milord."

"I'd be in seventeen kinds of bliss if I could do that, you know, Corky."

"I'm sure you would, milord."

"But I'd use a cricket bat rather than a rifle."

"Very right and proper, milord."

Though they then sank into contented silence for a few moments, their mood could not have been described as "relaxed". They had watched the movie many times, but never before with such concentration. Its content was a vital component in the plan they had hatched for the following day.

In *Chaps' Lonesome Stand* the hero had also decided to make his raid on the O'Connors' hideout very early in the morning. That should provide an element of

208

surprise. "THEY'LL BE DOZY WITH SLEEPING OFF THE EXCESSES OF THE NIGHT BEFORE" the caption read as he explained this to Tubby (though the point of explaining things verbally to a deaf-mute was one of the many questions the film did not address).

So Blotto and Corky Froggett also decided they would make their raid very early in the morning. The Lagonda purred its way out of the Hollywood Hotel garage at five-thirty.

At about the same time four hitmen stepped into cars parked outside separate anonymous Los Angeles apartments. Giovanni and Giuseppe also got into a black limousine parked outside Lenny "The Skull" Orvieto's HQ. They all knew where they were going. The Hollywood criminal grapevine had proved as efficient as ever. The hitmen's quarries would be found at the Barolo Brothers' hideout, where Twinks was being held and where Blotto was going to rescue her.

The Lagonda arrived first, and parked behind the shelter of some scrubby bushes, exactly where Chaps Chapple had tied up his faithful horse Lightning in *Chaps' Lonesome Stand*. Blotto, resolutely armed with his trusty cricket bat and feeling he had the strength of at least ten because his heart was so, so pure, stepped out of the car. Dawn was beginning to colour the sky grey, just as it had done in the monochrome movie.

"This is all creamy éclair," whispered Blotto as he and Corky crept across the rocky terrain towards the hideout's entrance. "I'm as sure as the favourite in a

209

one-horse race that this was the actual location used in the movie."

"I think you're right, milord. And having watched it only last night, we know the layout of the place precisely. Everything will work just like it did in *Chaps' Lonesome Stand*."

"Hoopee-doopee!" said Blotto.

Corky Froggett's prediction that everything would work out just like it did in *Chaps' Lonesome Stand* proved to be distressingly accurate. A moment later, as he rose to cross over to the shelter of another bush, a shot from inside the hideout hit Corky in the shoulder.

"Are you all right?" asked Blotto, just as Chaps Chapple's caption had asked in the movie. "Should I stay and look after you?"

Corky Froggett's head shook with just the same amount of vehemence as Tubby's had in the movie.

Blotto confused art with reality for a moment and said, just as Chaps' caption had, "You're a brave man, Tubby."

Then he zigzagged, cricket bat in hand, from sheltering bush to rocky cover, until he reached the narrow gap between the rocks which was the entrance to the Barolo Brothers' hideout.

He pressed himself close against the stone wall, confident that if he couldn't see the snipers above, then they couldn't see him either. At this point, he remembered, Chaps Chapple had lit a stick of dynamite and thrown it into the middle of the Barolo Brothers' natural fortress. But since dynamite was not one of the items available from the Hollywood Hotel's room service, Blotto had known he would have to use another approach. And he had come prepared.

After all, the only purpose of Chaps Chapple's stick of dynamite had been to create a diversion so that he could sneak into the hideout. And Blotto had his own way of creating a diversion, which he was convinced could not fail.

He had checked at the hotel that it was fully wound up and he knew this was its moment. Reaching into his pocket, he pulled out the clockwork jumping frog and threw it into the middle of the Barolo Brothers' compound. Then he rushed forward after it.

Whether anyone actually noticed the frog's presence is hard to tell. Certainly no one reacted to it. Blotto found himself looking down the barrel of a rifle, at the end of which was the leering face of Umberto.

Blotto looked round with some disappointment at the rocky amphitheatre in which he found himself. (It was three-sided so as to give access for the cameras.) Rodents, he thought, it's a bit beyond the barbed wire to change the set so much from the way it had been in *Chaps' Lonesome Stand*. Now there were fewer buildings in the space, just a wooden hut in the middle. Worse, there was no convenient pile of barrels visible. Nor was there a lifting apparatus attached to a beam on the side of a building. Nor a rope to swing down on.

Blotto was going to have to think of another way of mopping up the final remainder of the Barolo Brothers. If it worked as well as his substitution for dynamite of a clockwork jumping frog, the omens were not good.

Everywhere guns seemed to be trained on him. Not only was Umberto's rifle virtually up his nose, the ground level was full of Barolo Brothers with cocked revolvers. And high on the rocks looking down on them stood three men with automatic pistols.

Though Blotto usually welcomed having the odds against him, this went beyond a normal imbalance.

Umberto's grin had not got any less malevolent. "It is very generous of you to come here, Mr Lyminster. To save me the trouble of coming to get you. Your sister is already here, as a guest of the Barolo Brothers. And now it will give me great pleasure to kill both of you and brand your bodies with the 'BB' insignia of the Barolo Brothers!"

He cocked the rifle, which was only inches away from Blotto's chin. No need to worry about taking aim in a situation like that.

"Move round to your right," said Umberto. "I want all my Barolo Brothers brothers to see my revenge."

Blotto did as he was told, thinking that, well, he'd had a pretty good life, bit of a damper not finding his Holy Gruel by rescuing Mimsy La Pim, or Twinks come to that, but —

A shot rang out. Umberto dropped to the ground, dead.

Up on the rocks the Terminal Services hitman, who had had his automatic pistol trained on Blotto till the moment he moved, kicked himself. He tried to find his target again, but on the lower level all hell had broken loose. A fusillade of shots came towards him from the Barolo Brothers. Everyone seemed to be shooting without anyone being very clear what they were shooting at. Barolo Brothers fell like ninepins. The two other Terminal Services hitmen joined in the game.

Blotto had quickly decided that the only place where Twinks could be being held was the wooden hut, so he rushed towards it, knocking armed Barolo Brothers out of the way with his cricket bat.

He burst through the flimsy wooden doors to find Twinks facing him. Between them, with his back to Blotto, stood a man with an automatic pistol. Had he not been such a stickler for protocol, the results might have been very different, but the hitman was saying, ". . . and I thought you would like to know that your death will be the result of a contract taken out with Terminal Services, Los Angeles' most efficient organisation for —"

A downward stroke of the cricket bat (a shabby shot that would never have been tolerated at Lord's) felled the hitman in mid-flow. Blotto grabbed his sister by the hand. "Come on, Twinks me old toast-rack, let's get out of here like a pair of cheetahs on spikes!"

Outside the few men still standing kept up their unremitting fusillade. Again, nobody seemed too worried about who they were shooting at.

Soon Terminal Services would have to start the business of recruiting four new employees.

Because neither Blotto nor Twinks was armed, no one took any notice of them as they threaded their way through the throng to the narrow passage by which Blotto had entered the compound.

"Larksissimo!" said Twinks, as they gambolled down the rocky slope to the Lagonda. "You're a Grade A foundation stone, Blotters! I knew you'd come and rescue me in the nick of time!"

"How did you know that, Twinks?"

"Because you always do."

When they reached the Lagonda, they found that, in spite of his injury, Corky Froggett had dragged himself there and was lying on the ground beside it.

"Why didn't you get in, you voidbrain?" asked Blotto.

"I didn't want to spill my humble peasant blood on your aristocratic leather upholstery, milord."

"Don't talk such toffee, Corky. Twinks had better have a look at that shoulder of yours."

"Oh, don't you let the young mistress bother about something as unimportant as that, milord. It would be a great honour for me to die of gangrene in the service of the Lyminster family."

"You're talking complete meringue glacé," said Twinks. "You'll provide a much more useful service by getting better and being fit to drive again."

"If you say so, milady."

Twinks had cut through the fabric around the wound with a small pair of scissors, which she produced from her sequined reticule, and was now probing at the bloody hole with a delicate silk handkerchief. "Does that hurt, Corky?"

"Yes, milady, but a little pain in the cause of the Lyminster family is a small price to pay for —"

214

"Oh, Corky, for the love of strawberries, stuff a pillow in it! The bullet's still in the wound. It needs to be hoicked out quickly to avoid infection."

"Should we get him to a hospital?" asked Blotto anxiously.

"Don't don your worry-boots about that," his sister replied. "I can do it right here."

She reached into her sequined reticule and produced a set of surgical instruments, along with gauze, cotton wool, bandages and bottles of lotion. In no time she had removed the bullet, disinfected the wound and dressed it. Corky Froggett was made to lie, after many assertions that it wasn't his place to do so, across the back of the Lagonda.

"Tickey-Tockey," said Blotto, getting into the driver's seat. "So where do we pongle off to now — back to the hotel?"

Twinks sat down beside him. "Isn't there something you're forgetting, brother of mine?"

He looked puzzled. "Is there?"

"Mimsy La Pim."

"Great galumphing goatherds!" How could he have forgotten his mighty quest for the Holy Gruel? "Do you know anything about where she is?"

"Yes. She was locked up in the hut where I was."

"So you actually *saw* her?" asked Blotto, thunderstruck by the splendour of the idea.

"Yes, I did. And she told me what the Barolo Brothers were planning to do to her this morning."

"We know about that. Thanks goodness I got there in time."

"What in the name of snitchrags do you mean by that, Blotters?"

"The gunfight we've just escaped from must mean that she's all right. We just have to go back to the hut and get her. None of the Barolo Brothers will be left alive to take her off to the fumacious fate they'd prepared for her."

"If only life were that simple, Blotto. A bunch of the Barolo Brothers had driven off with her just before you arrived!"

The cloud of dust sent up by the Lagonda as it roared away was big enough to cause the weather stations of Los Angeles to warn of a potential tornado.

CHAPTER
TWENTY-SEVEN

Rescue!

Blotto and Corky's reconnaissance mission of the day before stood them in good stead as they knew exactly where they were going.

"And the stenchers told Mimsy what they were going to do to her, did they?"

"They spoffing well did, yes!"

"They don't deserve the name of human boddoes!"

"What's more, they said they were going to film the whole clangdumble."

"Why would they do that?"

"They said she'd lived so much of her life on screen, it made sense that her death should be on screen too."

"But why? What kind of leechworm would behave like that?"

"It's a turf war."

"What, you mean there are jockeys involved?"

"No, Blotto me old screwdriver. A 'turf war' is a war between rival gangs. Lenny 'The Skull' Orvieto and his family got to Hollywood first and started to control the criminal activity there. Then the Barolo Brothers arrived. They want to take over from him. There are rich pickings to be had in this town. But how do you put pressure on a man who's always surrounded by bodyguards? You can't get at him, so you kidnap his girlfriend."

"So she wasn't kidnapped for a ransom, after all?"

"Not the old jingle-jangle, no. In spite of what it said in the note. They just wanted power."

"And what about you? Were they going to ask for a ransom in good old spondulicks for you?"

Twinks's azure eyes hardened as she said, "I don't think so."

"So what kind of fate were they planning for you if . . .?" Blotto's words trickled away. He realised how lucky he had been to get to Twinks in time. He also realised how much his sister meant to him. For a moment he contemplated taking her hand or saying something mushy. But no, boddoes like him didn't go in for that sort of flim-flummery.

"We're getting close now, aren't we, milord?" said Corky Froggett. He could see enough from his recumbent position on the back seat to recognise the route they had travelled the day before.

"Yes, we are, by Denzil," the young master agreed.

"There was that little thicket near the embankment, milord, where we reckoned we could park up and get a view of what was going on."

"Which is exactly where I'm parking now," said Blotto, as he brought the Lagonda to a graceful halt in the appointed place.

"Off we go, by Denzil!" he shouted as he got out of the car. "To rescue Mimsy La Pim! Come on, Twinks!"

218

And, cricket bat in hand, he ran across the dusty field towards the embankment.

Twinks had a quick word with Corky Froggett, handed him something from her sequined reticule, and then ran fleetly to catch up with her brother.

The Lagonda had raised so much dust on the old dirt road that they hadn't been aware of the black limousine following them.

Giovanni and Giuseppe had arrived at the Barolo Brothers' compound a little after the four Terminal Services hitmen. Alerted by the sounds of gunfire, they had kept their distance until they were clearer about what was going on.

But when they saw Blotto and Twinks running down the hill to the Lagonda, they knew what they had to do. And they knew what Lenny "The Skull" Orvieto would do to them if they failed in their mission. In business matters Orvieto was a man of almost excessive probity. If he had taken out a contract on someone, it was a point of honour with him to see that the contractual obligations were fulfilled. And if any of his employees proved inadequate in the commission of those obligations, then contracts were immediately out on them too.

Giovanni and Giuseppe would not have risked going so close to the Lagonda if they had not seen Blotto and Twinks leave the vehicle and set off across the fields towards the embankment. As it was, they parked their black limousine right next door to it. They were not worried about its being discovered. While the two of them were going to come back to their car, there was no way that Blotto and Twinks would be coming back to theirs.

The two hoods once again checked their automatic pistols before emerging from the thicket and following the path taken by their quarries.

Completely unaware that their every move had been watched by the injured Corky Froggett in the back of the Lagonda.

Blotto knew exactly where he was going. The reconnaissance trip had not been wasted. They were at the location used by all the major Hollywood studios for tying-women-to-the-railway-line scenes.

As he crested the embankment slightly ahead of his sister, Blotto realised he had arrived only just in time. With their backs to him stood two of the Barolo Brothers desperados, watching what a third brother was doing down at the railway line. Three cameras were set up and already running. Again, Blotto couldn't help wondering what kind of stenchers would want to make a record of such a tragic scene. He wondered if the cameramen represented any danger to him and decided they didn't. They weren't part of the Barolo Brothers gang, just hired hands. Like most cameramen, so long as they were paid, they would shoot whatever their employers told them to shoot, no questions asked.

Already through the heat haze Blotto could see the approaching locomotive, travelling at huge speed, its triangular cow-catcher leading the way like the prow of a lethal ship. The volume of its engine roar grew as it came nearer, and the mounting rattle of the rails foretold its evil approach.

Then Blotto looked at the central focus of the scene. Mimsy La Pim chained to the railway lines. She was desperately mouthing her distress and pleading for mercy. She had played the scene so often in silent movies that it didn't occur to her to vocalise her terror now that the threat she faced was real.

Blotto knew he had to act fast. Putting a finger to his lips for Twinks's benefit, he then felled the thugs with their backs to him with two blows from his cricket bat. Before the third had time to draw his revolver, he was immobilised with an upward smash to the chin that sent him flying to the ground. (For purists, it should be noted that the first two strokes were unorthodox and would have caused pained wincing at Lord's, but the third was a perfect straight drive.)

"Manacle them," shouted Blotto to his sister, as he rushed down to the railway track.

Twinks extracted from her sequined reticule three sets of handcuffs and leg irons and had the Barolo Brothers thugs immobilised before any of them came to.

"Mimsy!" cried Blotto, finally seeing what he had come to Hollywood to see.

"Blotto!" cried Mimsy La Pim, remembering him well from their encounter in the South of France.

But this wasn't the moment to catch up on the minutiae of how they had both spent the intervening years. They had other, more pressing, priorities.

The vibration of the rails was now so ferocious, and the shriek of the approaching locomotive so loud, that Blotto realised he had only seconds to effect the rescue.

He knew that in some movies of the tying-women-to-the-railway-line genre, a cross-country race by the hero would lead to a message somehow reaching the engine room of the train and the grimy driver slamming the brakes on, so that the huge machine stopped within inches of its fair prey. But Blotto didn't think that scenario was in the script of the movie he was currently featuring in.

He wished for a moment that he had some more useful instrument than a cricket bat to break through the chains that imprisoned Mimsy. A pair of bolt cutters perhaps. But he remembered the words of one of his beaks at Eton who'd said, "It is the mark of an English gentleman that, in hostile foreign parts, he can always make do with what is to hand."

And a cricket bat was what Blotto had to hand.

Besides, he had another advantage — his strength was, after all, as the strength of ten because his heart was pure. He hooked the bat under the chains, gripped hard on each end and pulled upwards with a cry of, "I'm going to rescue you, Mimsy!"

The locomotive was now so close he could see the driver's eyes. There was no compassion in them, only cruel, evil purpose.

The cow-catcher was within inches of cleaving the pair of them in twain.

Suddenly Blotto's efforts were rewarded. The chains broke. Lifting Mimsy up bodily, Blotto wrapped his

222

arms around her and the pair of them rolled off the rails into the dust, nanoseconds before the monstrous locomotive screeched past.

Blotto had found his Holy Gruel!

CHAPTER
TWENTY-EIGHT

Gratitude

"OK," shouted one of the cameramen, "it's a wrap." With a lack of emotion that characterises their profession, he and the other two cameramen started to pack up their equipment.

Blotto and Mimsy La Pim both sat up, but he still kept his arms around her. He looked into her face and was, as when he'd met her for the first time, surprised by the pinkness of her cheeks and the redness of her lips. He had seen her so often in the movies that he expected her to be in black and white.

He smiled at her. "Close shave, but what some boddoes call 'a happy outcome', wouldn't you say?"

"No, I would not!" snapped Mimsy La Pim.

Blotto was so shocked by this reaction that he was momentarily deprived of speech.

"Why do you have to put your dumb fingers into pies where they ain't wanted?"

"What do you mean?" Blotto finally managed to ask. "Are you saying you didn't want me to rescue you?"

"Damn right I didn't! You cannot begin to know how much planning has gone into this caper. Lenny set it up for me."

"Lenny 'The Skull' Orvieto?"

"Of course Lenny 'The Skull' Orvieto. How many other Lennies are there that I happen to live with?"

"Toad in the hole!" said Blotto.

"Listen, dumbo, for this to work I had to persuade Lenny to drop his prejudices about them and work with the Barolo Brothers. Let me tell you, that took some negotiation. And it was all going smooth as a dream until you came and poked your aristocratic British nose into things."

"But why did you want Lenny to organise your kidnap?"

"Oh, come on! Don't you understand anything, beef-brain? We're in Hollywood. And what fuel does the whole Hollywood system run on? Publicity, baby, publicity. That's the only thing that's going to revive my career."

Blotto looked puzzled. "Look, I'm sure your being killed by a train would get a lot of publicity, but how's it going to help your career if you're dead?"

"I wouldn't be dead, knucklehead. Why do you think you found it so easy to break the chains with that stick you were carrying?"

"It is not a stick," said Blotto with lofty disdain. "It's a cricket bat."

"Cricket bat, stick — who's counting? Those chains were sawn through so a baby could break them. Why'd you think the cameras were set up? That footage was going to feature in the newsreels within days. Everyone in Hollywood would have seen it."

Blotto still wasn't keeping up. "Would have seen you being coffinated?"

"No! Would have seen me freeing *myself* in the nick of time. Roles for women are changing here in Hollywood. They don't want helpless innocents no more. Women in movies are getting more assertive. Independent. Footage of someone like me, who's been kidnapped by the notorious Barolo Brothers and still manages to escape their wicked plans *by my own efforts* . . . well, that'd put me in the frame for a whole lot of new independent female roles . . . maybe even in the talkies, if they ever actually happen."

"Hoopee-doopee," said Blotto, still a bit confused.

"But then you burst in like a football player at a quilting evening and the whole project's up the Suwannee. If you knew the harm you have just done to my career . . . The minute I tell Lenny about this . . . after all the dollars he spent on it, all the humble pie he had to eat to get the Barolo Brothers on board . . . you're a dead man. He'll put a contract out on you, that's for definite."

Neither of them realised, of course, that Lenny had already put the contract out. And that its specifications were yet to be met.

"A contract for what?" asked Blotto, suggesting that it wouldn't have made a lot of difference if he had known about it.

"You'll find out!" said Mimsy La Pim aggressively.

There was silence between them. Twinks, tactfully not wishing to intrude on their tête-à-tête, kept her

226

distance, standing guard by the three manacled Barolo Brothers.

Finally, Blotto said, "Well, it is creamy éclair to see you after all this time."

"I don't know what the hell you mean, but whatever it is, I can't say the same about you!"

"Fair biddles," said Blotto. Then, feeling that his quest should not be abandoned without at least a token struggle, he went on, "I was thinking, you know, now we have met again, Mimsy, it would be a beezer wheeze if we could spend a bit of time together and —"

"When hell freezes over, you klutz!" said Mimsy La Pim, as she stomped away from him and went to hitch a ride back to Hollywood with the cameramen.

Blotto would not have been the first knight errant who had discovered when, after much searching, he had found the Holy Gruel, it was not worth having after all.

Needless to say, it was Twinks who decided what they should do with the manacled Barolo Brothers. Frogmarching them over to the Lagonda and ferrying them back to Los Angeles sounded too much like hard work. So, reaching into her ever-resourceful sequined reticule, Twinks produced some chain links, with which she joined the three villains together. If they were able to move at all in their formation as a giant charm bracelet, they certainly wouldn't get far. And back at the Hollywood Hotel Twinks would alert the LAPD to their whereabouts.

Blotto was a little cast down as they walked from the railway to the Lagonda. His fantasies of being reunited with Mimsy La Pim had been with him for some years, and they had been nurtured by every new movie of hers he saw at the Tawsford Picture Palace. So some level of disappointment was understandable. Twinks did not say anything. She knew that her brother's fits of melancholy didn't last long, and that his natural buoyancy usually reasserted itself within minutes.

Twinks herself was feeling almost manically cheerful. Everything they could possibly have achieved in Hollywood had been achieved, except for the entrapment of a Texas oil millionaire, and having met one of those, she thought she was well out of any such liaison. Now there was nothing to stop them shaking the dust of Los Angeles off their feet and returning to Tawcester Towers as soon as possible.

They were both dreamy as they approached the Lagonda, Blotto ankle-deep in gloomy dreams, his sister deeper in cheery ones.

So they were quite surprised to hear an Italian-accented voice say, "Stop! You are about to take your last steps on this earth!"

They were equally surprised to be confronted by Giovanni and Giuseppe, both holding automatic pistols.

Blotto and Twinks looked at each other, their expressions echoing the same thought. This really was rather tiresome. After the shoot-out at the Barolo Brothers hideout and the unappreciated rescue of Mimsy La Pim, they'd really thought their morning's work was done. All either of them wanted to do was get back to the Hollywood Hotel for generous cocktails and a large lunch. Neither had much energy left to deal with two Italian hitmen.

They couldn't think of many ways of dealing with them, anyway. Giovanni and Giuseppe were too far away from them for Blotto to be able to do anything with his cricket bat, and the field in which they stood was empty of convenient rocks to hide behind.

Wearily, Twinks realised she'd have to resort to the old tactic, much used in such situations, of talking her way out of it. "Well, look it may tickle your mustard to kill us, but I do think you should have a little cogitette about —"

"Can it, lady!" said either Giovanni or Giuseppe.

Oh, snickets! Talking their way out of it wasn't going to work. In fact, it looked like nothing was going to work as the two Mafiosi raised their pistols and each took a bead on one of the siblings.

Blotto and Twinks held hands in a final gesture of solidarity.

Two shots rang out.

There was a moment of stillness, then, in unison, Giovanni and Giuseppe both fell forward onto the ground.

"Well done, Corky!" cried Twinks. "Give that pony a rosette! Lucky I gave you the Derringer, wasn't it?"

The chauffeur smiled. He had only been doing what he did best. He had been designed as a killing machine. And he had just killed in the cause of defending the Lyminster family, which made things even better.

CHAPTER
TWENTY-NINE

A New Star in the Hollywood Galaxy!

BRIT BEEFCAKE BIFFS HOLLYWOOD BIG-LEAGUERS IN RIP-ROARING RESCUE BID!

Once again your gal with fingers on more pulses than a pea-canning plant has an excluseroonie for my friends in fanland! You'll be seeing this on the newsreels soon, babes, but you heard it from Heddan first! Hollywood has a new hunk! Forget Toni Frangipani and Hank Urchief — their beefcake's crumbling and there's no contest in the face of the new cookie on the block. He's so darned good-looking it isn't fair on the rest of his gender. But he doesn't just *look* heroic, he *does* heroic too! We've all seen movies where maidens are rescued from massacre by locomotive in the nick of time, but now there's footage that flashes it up for real. Some minor moll with Mafia minders musta got on the wrong side of her mister, cos she found herself chained in the channel of a choo-choo. It was about to be thumbs-down for the dumb clown when Hollywood's new hero hitched her up to heaven, plucked her from the path of the chugger and rescued her rashers!

Before he's seen on your screens, only I, your newsie floosie Heddan, can be your guide to his ID. He's a bit of a Brit and his surname's the same as kidnapped cupcake Honoria Lyminster, who recently raised a riot by humiliating Hollywood's hunks and hitailing away from *The Trojan Horse*. Yes, the coming colossus is her brotheroonie Blotto — or to give him his noble name, Devereux Lyminster. Not only is he a hit in Hollywood, he's also heir to the throne of England — a publicist's dream! You heard it here first, but you gotta believe, star-spotters, you'll hear it a lotta times more. Devereux Lyminster is the new Hollywood highroller! Producers and agents, please form an orderly line to sign up Daring Dev!

More soon from your marvellous movie maven Heddan Schoulders!

The next morning there was a bigger crowd than ever before at the cricket pitch behind J. Winthrop Stukes's mansion. The match was the White Knights v. the Peripherals, Ponky Larreighffriebollaux's line-up of his old muffin-toasters from Eton. Stukes felt very pleased with himself for having secured the services of Blotto to play for the White Knights.

On this occasion Hank Urchief was not at the game. He was ensconced with his lawyer, trying to sue Terminal Services for breach of contract. Toni Frangipani and Wilbur T. Cottonpick were ensconced with their lawyers trying to do exactly the same.

Few of those present in front of the pavilion seemed to be aficionados of the game. Their only interest was when Devereux Lyminster was going to leave the field so they could talk to him. Having no knowledge of cricket, they couldn't understand that, because he was opening the batting for the White Knights, he would not return to the pavilion until he was out. And since he had played most of the Peripherals' bowlers at school from the age of about twelve, he knew all their little tricks and was in no danger of ever getting out. Six after six sailed over the various boundaries.

Twinks was there to watch, hugely relieved that the list of spectators included no amorous swains. Her Hollywood visit had included enough of those to last a lifetime. Though not particularly interested in what was happening on the pitch, she sat quite happily beside a recuperating Corky Froggett. His injury was causing him a little discomfort but he hardly felt it. He was still glowing with the satisfaction of having shot Giovanni and Giuseppe, fulfilling the destiny for which he had been put on God's earth.

On the other side of Twinks sat Ponky Larreighffriebollaux, watching his team's bowlers being humiliated by her brother. Tongue-tied as ever in her presence, he could manage little more than the occasional "Tiddle my pom!"

Eventually the morning session ended and lunch beckoned. Some of the other White Knights had succumbed to the Peripherals' bowling but, needless to say, Blotto had notched up another unbeaten century. Ponky's team were going to have to do wonders in the

afternoon to come close to the home side's total —
particularly if Blotto's prowess with the ball matched
what he had demonstrated with the bat. There was a
very contented smile on the face of J. Winthrop Stukes,
who always liked to lead a winning side.

When the crowd of non-cricket aficionados saw that
play had stopped, they rushed out onto the pitch to
besiege Hollywood's new hero with requests. Contracts
and pens were held out to him on every side.

"Mr Lyminster, I'm offering you an exclusive
ten-year contract with Humungous Studios . . ."

"Lyminster, Elephantine Studios will double any
offer made to you by those shysters . . ."

"Devereux, I'm directing a new movie about the life
of Abraham Lincoln and I'm sure you'd be perfect for
the leading role . . ."

"Dev buddy, you could have been born to play the
part of Napoleon in the new blockbuster I'm
producing . . ."

And so it went on, all the way back to the Pavilion.

Now Blotto had been very well brought up. He very
rarely expressed anger. His default mode was politeness
. . . sometimes patronising politeness when dealing with
inferiors, but politeness all the same.

This assault, though, was more than he could take.
And on the cricket pitch too! Did the stenchers have no
sense of propriety? He had been goaded beyond
endurance and, just as his sister had done, he found
himself resorting to strong language.

"Snubbins to the lot of you!" he shouted and went
into the pavilion to have his lunch.

CHAPTER
THIRTY

Home Sweet Home

Because of Corky Froggett's injury, Blotto did all the driving on the way back to New York. This was not something he minded. The irritation caused by having to drive on the wrong side of the road was partly compensated for by the emptiness of the road along which they drove. And the Lagonda was in its element. It loved lapping up the distance.

With every mile they put between themselves and Hollywood, Blotto felt less pained by the broken dreams he had nurtured about Mimsy La Pim. He hadn't had an opportunity yet to talk to Twinks about that situation, but when he did he would emphasise how clearly he had now come to distinguish between the world of the movies and real life.

He even wondered whether the benefit of having year-round cricket was sufficient compensation for the other things one had to put up with in Hollywood.

He only really had one regret about their American visit. He still didn't know when to say "got" and when to say "gotten". Except in *Gott in Himmel!*, of course.

Twinks was just as happy as her brother about the prospect of going home. From the moment she had left the place, she hadn't had a single backward thought about Hollywood or the collection of amorous swains she'd left there. Of course, she wasn't coming back with a Texas oil millionaire — something that might take some explaining to the Mater — but updating the Tawcester Towers plumbing would just have to wait.

She looked forward to being home. One of the first things she'd do would be to arrange a visit to Oxford to see Professor Erasmus Holofernes. After all the voidbrains she'd encountered in the movie world, it would be refreshing to engage with a proper intellect.

The surface of Hollywood closed after the departure of Blotto and Twinks without a ripple. Within a week Heddan Schoulders had tales of even newer stars to report. Yesterday's sensations were quickly forgotten.

So too were the bruisings received by Hank Urchief and Toni Frangipani. Time, the sycophancy of agents and producers, and the availability of infinite numbers of nubile starlets soon massaged their egos back to their customary supersize.

But as the prospect of talkies moved from rumour to reality, the chances of Toni Frangipani's career having a future evaporated. And whether Hank Urchief's beefcake charm would make the transition was also open to debate.

Gottfried von Klappentrappen's ability to adapt to the demands of making "talkies" was another unknown quantity, but in the meantime he continued to strut and bully his way about the set of *The Trojan Horse*. And he kept thinking of new elements to mix into the salmagundi of his plot.

For instance, he drafted Toni Frangipani into the cast to play Hannibal. And he would listen to no arguments to the effect that Hannibal and the Trojan War happened in different centuries. He just wanted to get some elephants into his movie.

Paul Uckliss-Hack, the writer, and Professor Gervase Blunkett-Plunkett, the classical adviser, tore out all of their remaining hair.

The Trojan Horse was now so far over budget that the accountants had stopped counting. It looked like Wilbur T. Cottonpick might achieve his aim of losing money on the movie. And as for his plan to lose money by introducing cricket to the USA, he finally gave the idea a firm "Nope."

On the domestic front, Gottfried von Klappentrappen divorced Zelda Finch. Cushioned by the large settlement she received, she decided to reinvent herself as an upmarket phobia therapist. There was always a demand for such services in Hollywood. Creating her own system of aversion therapy, she kept a tank of snakes in her consulting room. And nothing gave her greater pleasure than making clients with ophidiophobia handle them.

Her ex-husband married Buza Cruz next, but that only lasted a couple of weeks. In the limited time he had when he wasn't on the set of *The Trojan Horse*,

Heddan Schoulders assured her readers he was looking for wife number eight.

With the decease of all the Barolo Brothers, Lenny "The Skull" Orvieto found himself, for a while, the unrivalled king of crime in Hollywood. This made him relax in a way he never had before, and he found he had rather a taste for the quiet life. He married his long-term mistress Mimsy La Pim, who had given up acting, and together they took bridge lessons to fill the long hours of their comfortable retirement.

Terminal Services, faced with exorbitant law suits from Hank Urchief, Toni Frangipani, Gottfried von Klappentrappen and many other dissatisfied clients, went out of business. But there were still plenty of other places in Hollywood where hitmen could be found when required.

The Lagonda arrived back at Tawcester Towers late one evening. Moonlit frost gleamed on every crenellation of the huge building. English stars sparkled in an English heaven.

Blotto was back in a country where no cricket would be played until the following April, but he couldn't have cared less. In the morning he would go to the stables and reacquaint himself with his beloved hunter Mephistopheles. Riding to hounds and shooting every animal that moved would keep him going until the next cricket season.

In the morning he and his sister would also have to face the interrogation of the Mater in the Blue Morning Room, but that night, as they slipped into the familiar embrace of damp sheets and heard the reassuring clanking of the plumbing, both Blotto and Twinks were glad to be home.

Other titles published by Ulverscroft:

BLOTTO, TWINKS AND THE RIDDLE OF THE SPHINX

Simon Brett

Yet another financial crisis at Tawcester Towers! So this time the Dowager Duchess decides to sell off family possessions long consigned to the attic. Drawn to an Egyptian sarcophagus decorated with hieroglyphs, Twinks starts to translate: "Anyone who desecrates this shrine will be visited by the Pharaoh's curse . . . " just as the family chauffeur prises the lid off. The curse of the Pharaoh is now upon Corky, and it's up to Blotto and Twinks to travel to Egypt to banish it!

A NEST OF VIPERS

Andrea Camilleri

On what should be a quiet Sunday morning, Inspector Montalbano is called to a murder scene on the Sicilian coast. A man has discovered his father dead in his Vigàtan beach house: his body slumped on the dining-room floor, his morning coffee spilt across the table, and a single gunshot wound at the base of his skull. First appearances point to the son having the most to gain from his father's untimely death, a notion his sister can't help but reinforce. But when Montalbano delves deeper into the case, and learns of the dishonourable life the victim led, it soon becomes clear that half of Vigàta has a motive for his murder, and this won't be as simple as the inspector had once hoped . . .